D1251397

9-21

TRAILER
TRASH
HAVANA

JUNIO CAROLS

authorHOUSE®

AuthorHouse™ UK
1663 Liberty Drive
Bloomington, IN 47403 USA
www.authorhouse.co.uk
Phone: UK TFN: 0800 0148641 (Toll Free inside the UK)
         UK Local: 02036 956322 (+44 20 3695 6322 from outside the UK)

Published by AuthorHouse   01/22/2021

ISBN: 978-1-7283-7925-8 (sc)
ISBN: 978-1-7283-7924-1 (e)

Picture a campsite ideally situated between Altea and Albir on the Northern coast of Spain, overlooking an inviting blue-green sea. The locals like to call Havana, or Trailer Trash Pond Life. There are approximately twenty trailers, all occupied, and a small clubhouse, an office, and little else. (Who needs more?)

These trailers come in all shapes and sizes, some not much bigger than a rabbit hutch. The residents who reside here come from all walks of life, all characters in their own right.

This is a story of the trials, tribulations, and ups and downs of the unusual misfits who live (or exist) here.

AT THE FAR end of the campsite nestled number 20. There you could usually find Lucinda, still in her skimpy night attire, doing her first morning ritual. She was out on her decking feeding the entourage of wild ducks, birds, and the odd squirrel or two. Anything that remotely resembled an animal she would stuff with any leftovers available.

Lucinda sighed as she chucked the remains of last night's curry over the railing, thinking, *I hope their little bottoms can cope. Best fill the water barrel just in case. I'd better get back to my pigeonhole of a kitchen and get breakfast on the go before Roberto gets his grumpy bones out of bed.*

Lucinda was just slapping a rasher of bacon on the grill when Roberto burst into the kitchen.

'Hell's bells, Lucinda', Roberto said. 'Flash Harry next door is doing his usual parade of strutting up and down the decking in his budgie smugglers, fagging it, beer belly threatening to burst loose. For goodness sake, he's in his 70s. He looks like a sumo wrestler. Even the dog looks ready to lob up his breakfast'.

Lucinda looked out the kitchen window just as the wife, Lena, wafted out wearing her usual kaftan, looking like a bell tent. 'I hope she doesn't fart. She's likely to take off', she said.

She added, 'I think we'll abandon breakfast. I'm feeling a little nauseous. Let's go for a walk on the front, Roberto, mingle with normal people for a change instead of the circus freaks and nutters living here'.

Roberto shot off into the minuscule bathroom to bag the hot water first. 'Lucinda!' he shouted. 'Will you stop using my razor? It's full of hairs. I hope they aren't pubes', he added under his breath.

Lucinda sidled into the bedroom and looked at her meagre wardrobe. Sighing, she said, 'There just isn't room for many clothes—hardly enough room for a double bed'.

When they first moved here, downsizing (you could say that again), she'd had to give most of her clothes to charity. Mind you, when the majority were bought from Giorgio Asada, it didn't seem such a great loss, she thought.

Roberto burst into the boudoir smelling like a floral display, totally naked, huffing and puffing, complaining about the bathroom being like a sauna. 'If you opened the windows', he said, 'the neighbours have a bird's eye view'.

Lucinda muttered, 'I'm sure they've seen better specimens on the beach'.

Roberto couldn't make his mind up whether to wear his blue shirt with the ducks or the pink one with the flamingos. 'Lucinda, which goes better with my khaki shorts?'

Lucinda groaned. Roberto had no dress sense at all. Anyone with style knows you don't pair pink and blue with khaki. She didn't want Roberto showing her up, if by chance they bumped into Jacques and Joyce, who owned the flash villa with the indoor and outdoor pools. Lucinda had been lucky enough to meet Joyce at the local spa and massage centre, which Lucinda frequented once a week.

Joyce and Lucinda hit it off straightaway. They had so much in common: good manners, impeccable dress sense, and they both enjoyed the Swedish massage that Enzo the Physiotherapist offered as his speciality. Not only was he drop-dead gorgeous, he liked to flirt with Lucinda, which made her feel special.

Lucinda blushed when she remembered when she and Roberto had been invited to Joyce and Jacque's pool party, getting to mingle with posh people for a change. Everything was going swimmingly until Roberto doffed off down to his speedos and jumped in the pool, splashing water all over Lucinda's bikini, which wasn't meant to get wet because it became see-through. Luckily she had thrown her kimono on, so no one noticed.

Roberto was impatiently pacing up and down. 'Sod it. I'll wear the pink one', he said, thinking Lucinda was in a trance again. *I wonder who this week's flavour of the month is. She's so fickle. Whoever seems to be splashing the most compliments and money about suddenly becomes her best mate.*

'Lucinda, snap out of it, or we'll be too late for the all-you-can-eat buffet at the Casino Royal. They stop serving at 11.30 and it's now 10.15. It takes at least twenty minutes to get there'.

Lucinda groaned. How humiliating to be seen at an all-you-can-eat buffet. Why can't we go to Lorenzo's tapas bar on the seafront? Such a better clientele there—not to mention the size of the *gambas al ajillo* (garlic shrimp) she could wash down with a light rosé wine.

HARRY COUGHED AND spluttered for at least ten minutes. 'Too many fags for breakfast', he muttered. 'And maybe finishing that last bottle of plonk didn't help'.

He shook his head. 'Oh sod it, whatever gets you through your day. Hey, Yellow', he said to his mutt of a dog, aptly named because of his colour, a lovely shade of nicotine (not sure what colour he should have been).

Lena put her arm (bingo wings in full swing) loosely round Harry's shoulder, rasping in his ear, 'Boy do I feel rough. Must have been that dodgy burger last night', and gave an almighty burp.

Harry scoffed. 'So it had nothing to do with the six gins, four tequilas, and a brandy chaser then'.

Lena quickly rasped back, 'You didn't do so bad yourself, swigging down a litre of local plonk'.

Harry growled and shouted to Yellow, 'What the hell you looking at, mutt? Get inside now. Smirking at me like that. Don't judge me or you'll be eating squirrel poo for a week'.

Lena wafted back inside, leaving the distinct aroma of sweat, booze, and fags, stepping into their brown-stained kitchen, nicotine flavoured and smelling like a tramp's armpit.

Lena was always too tired to clean—and anyway, she always said to herself, 'It will only get dirty again. My health comes first. Now where did I leave my fags and that glass of sangria?'

Lena shouted back outside to Harry, 'Can you bring my ashtray in? It's on the glass table out there. This one inside is full and that one is empty'. She grabbed her glass, which was smeared with dirty fingerprints, heavily dropped her bulk on the settee, and switched on the TV to watch *The Young Doctors* abroad.

She could daydream about her being one of the young nurses being serviced by one of the doctors—not to be choosy, any would do.

Harry swore, 'That lazy bitch', under his breath. 'Too fat and lazy to get it herself. Who does she think I am, her waiter?' He snatched up the ashtray and flounced inside, puffing and panting, mumbling, 'How demanding she is'.

He was wasting his breath. Lena was in total rapture, looking at the TV screen.

Not bloody doctors again, he thought. *She has a fetish for the medical profession.*

Harry stormed back outside just in time to shout hello to Lucinda and Roberto as they tried to sneak past his tin hut without being seen.

'Stuck-up pair', Harry muttered. 'I'll bet she's all fur coat and no knickers. She needs a good seeing to'. Although he did feel sorry for Roberto.

Roberto was a workaholic who trundled off every day to his local news office, where he printed all sorts of local gossip and idle chitchat for the local rag. Harry didn't blame him for escaping Lucinda's constant nagging and shouting, 'Have you done this and that?' all day long.

Harry was jolted back to reality by a loud smash inside his tin hut. 'Shit', he said, 'I bet Lena's in a drunken stupor again and dropped her bottle of tequila'. *Note to self: start buying plastic bottles.*

Harry shot back inside weary of what he was going to find, he nearly tripped over yellow who bolted out of the door. 'What the 'eff' is going on, Lena? What have you smashed now?'

Lena said, 'Shush, Harry. You're interrupting my viewing. It's only your aftershave bottle you left on the coffee table. I spilt a bit of my vino, which happened to land on Yellow, startling him. He jumped up and the table tipped over'.

Harry smelled a mixture of Old Spice mingled with booze, fags, and sweat. He went into the kitchen to fetch the brush and pan, otherwise the broken glass would remain there indefinitely; he didn't want Yellow getting glass in his paws. All he needed now was a huge vet bill. He was struggling enough to keep Lena in fags and booze, not to mention the mountain of food she managed to polish off.

Lena put the TV on hold. 'How am I supposed to concentrate when you keep faffing about under the table? just leave it till later—the queen isn't about to pay a visit, or anyone else for that matter. I can't remember the last time we had visitors, Harry'.

Harry muttered, 'Fat chance of that in this shithole'. Thinking, *If Lena isn't drunk as a skunk then I usually am—shame we're never sober together*. Bedroom frolics were a thing of the past. The only thing he could get hard these days was the bunion on his foot.

3

JEFF WAS SPYING out his blinds. His view overlooked Harry and Lena's decking (worst luck), and he didn't want to venture out for his daily spliff in case Lena was out parading her bulk around in her skimpy underwear. More like plus fours, with a hammock to keep up her enormous boobs.

Jeff thought they would be happier locating to a nudist site, save money on clothes.

As luck would have it, she had just wafted inside her smoking room (the kitchen), so he shot out, desperate for his fix.

Whilst taking his first drag of the day, his mind wandered to Dolly, his cleaning lady, who turned up once a week to clean his small trailer. Dolly was most likely in her 50s, but even though Jeff was pushing 70, he still thought he could make the earth move for her.

Dolly didn't mind him pinching her bottom, or pushing 5.00 euro notes down her ample cleavage, where he left his hands to linger a little longer than necessary.

Even though Jeff's trailer was no bigger than a rabbit hutch, Dolly always took her time, very thorough—but it was more likely to do with him always having a bottle of gin handy, plus extra spliffs.

Jeff knew he was trapped in this trailer park, because he couldn't afford to live anywhere else. But on the plus side, there was always a floor show going on somewhere, never a dull moment. Just like the Toby Keith song says, "There's always something going on down in the trailerhood." Jeff new everyone in the trailer park. He was the longest resident there. He knew he had a reputation as a lady killer.

In his youth, he had no trouble juggling two or three ladies at once; his stamina knew no bounds.

Jeff thought, *I know I'm no oil painting, but I still have my cheeky charm, but it would be nice to lose a couple of stone, so I can say hello to parts of my anatomy I haven't seen in a while.*

He wished he had the funds to go out more, meet some willing ladies looking for fun, but money was tight, and you know what they say—if it had wheels, tits, or floats, you'll always be skint.

Oh well. He would just have to look forward to his weekly grope with Dolly for now. Maybe talk her into taking him to her bingo class, her treat. It was one way to try to replenish his moth-eaten wallet.

Jeff was just taking a long drag on his spliff when Gabby waved at him from her decking. He waved back with a smile.

Gabby was OK. She had a kind heart, just a bit too needy, and she didn't mind letting him know. Not too sure if he was strong enough to cope with Gabby just yet—he didn't like forceful women. His wife, Gail, had been too pushy and demanding (a shame not in the bedroom), otherwise they would still be married instead of going through a bitter divorce. She ended up with the bungalow, the car, and his prized collection of records.

Even the solicitor said to him, 'Why would you want to keep anything that would remind you of that bitch?'

Jeff agreed, so he ended up in a tin hut you couldn't swing a cat in, and no car, just shanks' pony. Luckily, Dolly didn't mind doing him a weekly grocery shop—worth her weight in gold, that one.

4

CASSY WAS SAT on her sun lounger overlooking the beach, people watching, her favourite sport. She sighed as she watched a lithe female playing volleyball. If only she had the stamina or energy to just go for a walk, it would be a start. However, this was not going to happen. Her bulky frame and weak legs dictated that she had to use a mobility scooter if she wanted to go anywhere.

Cassy sometimes got very upset or angry when she caught the neighbours eying her up. She knew that behind her back they called her Mama Cass, with an overactive fork, and why hadn't she tried to lose weight?

Cassy had been big since she was young and was diagnosed with an underactive thyroid and a genetic defect. Her mother was huge. Cassy practically lived on rabbit food, to no avail.

She said to herself, 'Let's hope I don't get cravings that rabbits get, always at it.' Her husband, Jimmy, would love that. Although he would have to do all the work, while she just lay there.

Cassy said, 'I know I'm a good person, always willing to help others, and I'm good company. I love a good laugh. So stuff the miserable, nosy gits who judge me'.

Jimmy loved her just as she was. He'd married her when she was big. They say true love is blind.

Cassy turned her head away from the beach babes and looked towards Willie's trailer, which slightly overlooked her decking.

Willie was waving and shouting at her to see if he could come over for a coffee and a gossip.

Cassy laughed and nodded. Willie might be overly camp, but he was good for a laugh and lots of new gossip.

Jimmy took Cassy's morning coffee out to her and gave her a quick peck on the cheek. 'I'm just off to work, love. Is there anything you need me to bring back later?'

'Yes. I've run out of G&Ts, so be a love and get me some'.

Jimmy made a mental note and set off down the path to exit at the end. He worried that Cassy was getting too dependent on her G&Ts, but then he thought, *Bugger. Whatever gets her through her mundane day is OK with me.* Anyway he liked a tipple or two himself, but everyone knew you don't mix the hops with the vine, because that's a fool's game.

He remembered the one time he had indulged in a whisky chaser. He had a heavy metal group banging away in his skull. He'd had to take the day off work, at the mercy of Cassy, not his idea of fun.

What was that saying going round his head? "Whisky makes you frisky, and beer makes you queer". True, but better not say this in front of Willie and his partner Nobby.

Cassy heaved her bulk out of the chair. *Better put the kettle on and get the Garibaldis out,* she thought. *Willie is rather partial to those. Hope he doesn't bring Nobby, he'd just spoil a good gossip by always turning the conversation around to him.* She couldn't abide Nobby to be in the limelight.

Cassy noticed her bottle of Gordon's was nearly empty, thinking, *I hope Jimmy gets back with my gin before 6pm, otherwise I'll be climbing the walls.*

*

Jimmy arrived at work fifteen minutes later at the waterpark where he worked. He made a beeline for the little cafe for his morning coffee before he had to cope with the onslaught of all the little brats running around screaming, spraying water and debris everywhere.

Jimmy sighed as he entered the café. Sat slurping her caffeine intake was Kelly, her wild red hair tied up like a lion's mane. She had trowelled her make-up on, tarted up to the nines, her curvy legs crossed, revealing plump thighs. Jimmy had fantasies about Kelly, which he kept to himself, until he was alone and his hands were free.

Kelly smiled, red lipstick smudged on her top teeth. 'Hi, Jimmy', she said. 'How's Cassy?' (All the time she was thinking, *Jimmy deserves better, he's so thin, and she's like a beached whale*.)

Kelly knew she was no skinny-Minnie, but she liked to think of herself as voluptuous, with everything in proportion. Men liked something to get hold of, not a bag of bones.

She liked to flirt with Jimmy just enough to keep him on the back burner for now. She knew her fling with Julio, the boss of the waterpark, was about to fizzle out. Julio's wife was getting suspicious, turning up unexpectedly at inappropriate moments.

She'd nearly caught them in a compromising position last week while Kelly and Julio were having a fumble behind the ice cream hut. They heard Julio's wife say, 'I'll have a 99 with two flakes, please'.

Julio shot off struggling to fasten his trousers, rounding the other side of the hut, colliding with two brats, who spilled their slushy all down his flies. *Try explaining that to the wife*, she'd thought.

She had quickly dived on to the floor pretending to look for an earring, knowing full well that she didn't have pierced ears.

Luckily, Julio's wife was too interested in licking her flake and shuffled off towards the water rafting.

Kelly sighed, thinking this maybe was the end of their fun. *Oh well. I'm going to have to work my charms on Jimmy, which shouldn't take long.*

Jimmy was asking Kelly if she would mind working until 6pm, so he could jet off early to the Smart Mart to get Cassy's gin. He didn't want to arrive home too late with it, or she would be in a foul mood otherwise.

Kelly gave him her full, cheesy grin. 'Yes, Jimmy, I'll do it just for you, but Cassie's treating you like a doormat. It's time you grew a pair.'

Jimmy didn't reply. She had hit the nail on the head— if only he could run off with Kelly into the sunset.

5

NOBBY WAS JUST putting the last cherry on his fairy cakes, looking very pleased with himself. *Dicky will be impressed. Best I've baked yet*, he thought.

Nobby baked all sorts of treats for Dicky's restaurant, and in exchange he and Willie ate for free there twice a week.

Nobby heard the door creaking and looked out the window. Willie was sneaking down the stairs on the decking, wiggling his pert bum towards Cassy's trailer.

As soon as Jimmy was out of sight, you could put money on Willie hotfooting over there to talk Chinese whispers.

'Oh well', mumbled Nobby, 'At least Cassy is the wrong sex to worry about, It would be entirely different if Willie was sneaking off to chat with Harry'. He had no one to blame but himself for always being left out of their conspiracies, although he was always welcome at

Jimmy and Cassy's—they sometimes all got together for a barbie and drinks.

Nobby didn't really drink much—it didn't agree with him because he had really bad acid reflux and curries and most spices he just couldn't tolerate. So he wasn't invited to a lot of evening meals out because they mostly liked to go to Indian restaurants. (Little did Nobby know this was one of the reasons they chose Indian—so he wouldn't come, due to him being an egotistical bore.)

Nobby knew he liked to brag about his past, present, and future. He felt a class above most of the trailer trash living here. He had built up his own empire through sheer hard work—and a little help from wealthy parents.

Nobby liked to spoil Willie with expensive gifts and designer clothes, not realising a trailer park was not really the right ambience to be seen wearing them. Nobby said to himself, 'I know I'm a snob, but they can either take me or leave me. Doesn't bother me that I'm not as popular as Willie. I like being a loner'.

Nobby went into the tiny bathroom, looked at himself in the mirror, and said with a sigh, 'I think those few grey hairs make me look very distinguished. I'm one of the lucky ones. I have it all: looks, money, and I'm an intellectual to boot'.

Nobby loved classical music, and watching movies (the old black and white films had so much going for them). Youngsters of today are only interested in sex and violence.

He knew Willie didn't enjoy the same kind of things he did, probably because he was a lot older, by far, but they both loved their holidays, going away at least three or four times a year to exotic destinations.

Willie was out on the decking, having a crafty fag out of Nobby's view. He knew if Nobby caught him, all hell would break loose.

Willie could visualise him shaking his finger, going red in the face, and shouting, 'Do you want to shorten your life by puffing on cancer sticks? And don't worry about me being a passive smoker—cough, cough, I have more respect for my lungs'.

Willie smiled. If only Nobby knew how many fags he'd lit up at Cassy's yesterday, not to mention the umpteen number of vinos he'd washed them down with, he'd most likely have a heart attack.

Willie enjoyed sneaking over to Cassy's he could be as camp as he wanted, just be himself. Cassy was like his mum, accepted him as he was, warts and all.

Willie knew from an early age he was gay, that girls did nothing for him, but he tried really hard to change. He had tried to lose his virginity to the local biker chick Sammy, but he just couldn't get a hard-on, no matter how he tried. Sammy luckily put it down to nerves and said they would try again soon. No chance of that every happening.

Willie tried very hard to keep his sexual preference hidden from his parents. The crunch came when his mum burst into his bedroom, without knocking and caught him with his tongue down some tarquin's throat. He was 17 at the time. His mum nearly fainted and took the stairs two at a time to get away from what she'd seen.

Bless her little cotton socks she never told his dad, and when he was alone with her, she'd smiled and put her hand on his, and said, 'Willie, I'll always love you, my son, so whatever floats your boat is fine by me. Promise me though you won't let your father know; it would kill him. Maybe make up a pretend girlfriend to fool him'.

Therefore, he used to take Milly a school friend, home for tea once a week, just to keep the peace. Little did his dad know Millie preferred girls, just as Willie preferred boys.

Willie moved out a couple of months later. Milly had got a steady girlfriend by then, so it was a godsend when his mates Tristram and Julian where going to share a flat in Brighton and needed a third party to help with the bills. Although they were a couple and shared a bedroom, and Willie had a bedroom to himself, they still split the bill three ways.

The three had a whale of a time out on Brighton front, frequenting all the nightclubs and bars until throwing out time. He never felt like a gooseberry; they always made him feel welcome.

But life has a way of putting obstacles in your way when you are having too much fun. Willie got a tearful call from his mum, sniffling down the phone, saying, 'Willie your dad has found out you are shacking up with two gays, and he's disgusted'.

He never spoke to Willie again, right up until the day he died, telling Willie's mum he didn't want him at his funeral. *Let him rot in hell, the bigoted fart.*

Willie had been offered a job at the Bird's-Eye View nightclub, which he jumped at, and although it would mean giving up his all-night partying, he would be earning his keep. He knew he would enjoy mingling with the punters, and friendly staff; they were all tied with the same brush.

Willie had just successfully finished his six-month probation when the owner of the club—Nobby—made an unexpected visit. Although he was a lot older than Willie, he charmed the pants off him.

Nobby decided a few months later that he wanted to retire, sell off his clubs, and travel all over. He was looking for a bolt hole (hence the trailer in Spain) to keep popping back to and wanted to spend, spend, spend.

The exciting thing was he wanted Willie to join him, and the rest, they say, is history.

Nobby proposed in Venice as they were floating on a gondola down a slightly smelly canal.

Willie had an overpowering urge to burst into song: 'Just one Cornetto, give it to me'.

They cemented their civil partnership at the local registry office and arrived back at the trailer as Mr and Mr Nutts.

*

Willie sighed, wondering where all the magic went. Slowly over the past ten years they had been here. Nobby had changed. He wasn't the fun-loving, spontaneous, wine-drinking, carefree guy he had married.

He wished Nobby would take the hint about why Willie was always eager to sneak over to Cassy's. He needed excitement, stimulation, fags, and booze, plus the latest gossip.

That reminds me, he thought. I must go tell Nobby about who was seen crawling out of Gabby's trailer the other night. He won't believe it.

*

Nobby looked up from his daily paper when Willie came breezing in, smelling slightly of fags. Nobby thought, *How many times must I tell him he's putting another nail in his coffin? At this rate he'll go before me, and I've got at least fifteen years on him!*

'Well,' said Nobby, 'how many did you smoke this time? Just the one, or one after another?'

Willie sighed. 'I do try, Nobby. It's just so boring doing nothing with my hands'.

Nobby smiled slyly. 'Oh, I could think of a few things that your hands would be good at'.

6

PEDRO WAS UNLOCKING the mail room, ready for the onslaught of the great unwashed busybodies (as he called them) known as trailer trash.

Gabby was the first to come busting in through the door, whinging and complaining about her leaky shower.

Pedro wished he could just tell her to bugger off. Instead, he took a deep breath, sighed, and mumbled, 'I've been too busy sorting out the blocked drains. Some bast*rd kept flushing sanitary products down the toilet, bloody women. This lot are worse than gypsies. I should know—I am one'.

Gabby rolled her eyes, and said, 'Not one you can pin on me. I went through the change years ago'.

Pedro held up his hand and said, 'Whoa, too much info. Your job is next on the list, I promise'.

Gabby banged the door shut on her way out. *What a waste of space Pedro is, his promises meant jack shit,* (nothing) she thought.

Pedro had no intention of fixing Gabby's shower. Instead, he'd send Juan, his handyman—in more ways than one. Gabby was so needy and made it bloody obvious she was always in heat.

The last time he'd gone to do odd jobs on her trailer, she'd found any excuse to rub her enormous boobs up against his arm, breathing heavily down his neck, whispering how she could do with a strong man like him around the place, dropping little hints of how lonely she was, how she had a lot of love to give to the right man.

Pedro was out in a flash—he definitely wasn't the right man. Gabby was not his cup of tea: big and blowsy with a loud mouth.

Pedro had pretended not to listen to the gossipmongers when they were in the mailroom, but his ears did prick up when Elvira was spouting off about who she had seen sneaking out of Gabby's trailer in the early hours of the morning.

Pedro happened to look up just as Elvira was looking at him. He knew he was a loudmouth bolshy bugger who didn't give a toss about the motley crew who lived in the trailers. His job was to man the office, collect bills, and do repairs, not service old boilers.

Anyway, he was trying to get back with his ex-wife, who had left him two years ago. She caught him with his trousers down, literally, servicing his secretary over his desk.

Sammy his wife was no saint either, she couldn't keep it in her pants (his handyman could vouch for that), so they were even. He didn't want any idle gossip getting back to her, especially if it involved Gabby.

Pedro coughed loudly, and Elvira and a few others looked at him. He said, 'Don't even think I would touch Gabby, not with a barge pole. She's fat, frumpy, and goodness knows what sexual nasties she has, so bugger off, all of you'.

Pedro looked at the clock, wishing it was closing time so he could lock up and get back to his laptop to finish watching *Debbie Does Dallas*. He thought, *Now there's a women I could do something for. I'll check the beer in the cooler, pop the pizza in the microwave, slip into something more comfy, and have a long-awaited reunion with Mrs Palm and her five lovely daughters.*

GABBY WAS JUST applying her ruby-red lipstick when she glimpsed a shadow pass her bathroom window out of the corner of her eye. She hoped it was Pedro or Juan come to fix her shower,.

I wish I was wearing something more inviting, she thought. *I'm really none too fussy which one turns up. I'd jump on either of their bones right now—I'm feeling a little horny.*

Gabby ran her brush through her unruly, bleached-blond curls and shot off outside, ready to flirt with whomever.

How disappointing it was only Flash Harry, shouting for Yellow, his mutt. She shuddered. Harry would be the bottom of the barrel, looking like the wild man of Borneo and smelling like a gorilla's armpit. Yuck.

Harry growled hello and licked his cracked lips, looking Gabby up and down, making a point of undressing her with his eyes.

Gabby quickly pulled her cardigan tighter to hide her chest. She didn't want him getting an eyeful of her cleavage, giving him ideas above his station.

Gabby knew she had a reputation for entertaining gentlemen (if you could call the motley bunch that), but she had a high sex drive and usually wasn't too choosy. Harry, she thought, would definitely be scraping the bottom of the barrel, and she would have to dip him in bleach first.

Harry lingered a bit longer than needed. He knew Yellow had strutted back on to the decking, but he wanted to make an impression on Gabby. She had earned her reputation as being loose with her favours. Harry was turned on by big women, and Gabby was big everywhere—boobs, bum—something to get hold of. She must be good in the sack. George one of Harry's oldest mates, could hardly walk after a session with Gabby, telling everyone she was like the Tasmanian devil.

Gabby knew she was no spring chicken and maybe gave the impression of being desperate for a man. She was, but it didn't stop them beating a path to her door. The wives should be grateful she was servicing their needs, which gave them respite from having to perform.

Gabby hid behind the shed until Harry slumped back inside, looking dejected. She almost felt sorry for him, not getting his oats at home.

'Phew', she said, 'that was a narrow escape'. *Hello,* she thought. *That looks like Juan's jeep coming down the path. I'd better slip into something more appropriate for seduction; you never knew your luck. I might be taking my attire off quicker than I put it on—here's hoping.*

Juan pulled up outside Gabby's and shrugged, thinking, *I hope she lets me fix the shower before she tries to molest me. Maybe I could drop a hint that I'm on medication due to having a dose of something down below.*

Twenty minutes later, Gabby's trailer could be seen rocking gently to and fro. Looked like Juan just made Gabby's day.

8

ELVIRA WAS FRANTICALLY trying to open six cans of cat food whilst juggling too many bowls out of her spartan cupboard. At her feet, eight felines where yowling and jumping all over the place, trying to get to the meaty chunks that stunk like a sewer.

'Bugger me', she said whilst listening to slurping and chomping around her. 'I'm starving, and all I have left in the fridge is a piece of mouldy cheese and a dry crust'.

I must do a shop, she thought, but after supplying her babies with their animal derivatives, there was only a meagre pittance left to supply her food.

There's only two options left. One, I ask for a pay rise, or two, I find myself a rich fella, she thought.

Sighing, she said to herself, 'I've more chance of the latter. Mr Moggie, my boss at the pet shop makes Scrooge look like Mother Teresa. Even if I turn up naked, he'd be totally oblivious. He only has eyes for young

Timmy, who helps out a couple of days, cleaning out the cages. Ugh, Moggie is old enough to be his grandfather'.

Elvira thought, *It might be my lucky night tonight. Dicky from number seven might be having his tea time tipple in the camp bar before heading off to work. I think I'll wear my tiger skin all-in-one, with the plunging neck. That should get any hotblooded male raring to go.*

Dicky must be worth a bob or two, she thought. *He owns the bistro next door to the clubhouse. He's a lot older than I'd like, and he has a slight squint, but if his wallet's healthy, I'm in.*

Elvira had no intentions of sitting in his bistro alone. *That's for sad losers,* she thought. She wanted Dicky to think she had lots of admirers dying for her company either in or out of bed.

Elvira knew most of the women (battle axes) on the campsite. They were extremely jealous of her voluptuous figure, piercing green eyes, and fake boobs. (Little did she know those battle axes thought she'd had Botox and used cat wee for perfume.)

Elvira also knew they called her crazy cat lady, as well as Chesty Morgan.

Funny how most of their husbands couldn't take their eyes off Elvira. *I'll bet they played with themselves under the table when I was at the bar.*

Elvira did not want other people's castoffs, especially when most of them had one foot in the grave and no money to leave behind. She was going to take the bull by the horns tonight and have a couple of chases for Dutch courage, and flirt openly with Dicky, hoping he lives up to his name.

Yowl! Yelp! She'd just stood on Bubbles and Tobias's tails, dreaming of what was to come.

JAVIER WAS WALKING past Elvira's trailer, humming on his way to rehearsal when he saw Elvira sashaying past the patio doors, not a stitch on. Javier nearly upchucked his Cheerios. Did Elvira know everyone called her buenos knockers (good-time gal)?

Javier walked as fast as he could, which wasn't easy in these high-heeled boots. He adjusted his long auburn wig, which complemented his tiger-skin backless sundress.

Javier hated being called a tranny—he was a transvestite. He loved dressing in women's clothing, even down to the peekaboo bra and thong. Javier was unsure about his sexuality. He was turned on by both sexes if they were eye candy and well spruced. *Wait until they see my creation I'll be wearing tomorrow for the pantomime.*

He was on his way to dress rehearsal at the town hall. Tickets had more or less sold out. Javier hoped he could do justice to the character of Priscilla from the musical *Priscilla, Queen of the Desert.* He'd been practising day and night to get it perfect.

Javier loved acting. It gave him a thrill to become different people all the time. That way he didn't have to dwell too much on his sad life, his struggle to find out who he really was, and what he wanted out of life.

Javier arrived at the town hall thirty minutes early. He wanted to check he had the right make-up for his sensitive skin. He couldn't just slap any old stage make-up on; it had to be hypoallergenic and organic. Last time he plastered foundation all over, he woke up the following morning with his face looking like the moon's surface.

I'll just pop backstage, he thought, *and have a quick browse of the costumes to make sure Barry and Burt's dresses don't outshine mine.* After all, he was the star of the show, so he needed to be the dazzling one.

Satisfied everything was looking good, Javier decided to do some limbering up and voice exercises. He sang scales—'Do-re-mi-fa-so-la-ti'—and went into his version of "My Way".

The town hall door was slightly ajar, and in burst a few shady lads from the campsite, sniggering and laughing, shouting, 'Hey, Nancy boy, how many of Elvira's cats did you step on to make that caterwauling? Go get yourself neutered'. They all ran out quickly as Javier's boot collided with the door.

Javier sighed. *It's difficult being famous and different. You rake up a lot of jealousy*, he thought. *Nevertheless, the show must go on.* 'Where was I?'

10

DICKY WAS BUSY doing a quick inventory of his booze shelf at his restaurant, wondering if he needed to nip to the Smart Mart for more whisky, when in walked Nobby carrying a big cake tin.

Dicky fairly salivated when he peeked into the tin at Nobby's delicacies he'd brought for the sweet cabinet.

'Wow. They look good enough to eat. Quick, put them over there in the cabinet before I blow my diet—no carbs for me for a while, I'm getting a bit of a paunch'.

Nobby looked at Dicky's protruding belly, and thought, *More like a beer barrel.* Dicky could drink anyone under the table.

Dicky jumped up and said, 'I'll make us a latte, and you can fill me in on what you've been up to'.

Dicky had a lot of time for Nobby. They had so much in common. Nobby used to be in the service trade, and Dicky still was. They had spent many an hour discussing stories of their antics and conquests over the years.

After Nobby left, Dicky couldn't understand what Willie and Dicky had in common. Those two were like chalk and cheese. They do say opposites attract—but couldn't be further from the truth with those two.

Dicky looked longingly at Nobby's fairy cakes and looked down at his portly belly. 'Willpower, Dicky, if you want to get to first base with Elvira. The paunch will have to go. Looks like carrot sticks again for lunch'.

Dicky was daydreaming of a Caribbean cruise with Elvira soaking up the sun on deck, with her skimpy bikini on, or even better, topless.

The door opened and in walked Roberto, looking slightly stressed.

'What can I do for you, Roberto?' Dicky asked, shaking himself out of his fantasy.

Roberto fidgeted a little and said, 'It's my wife, Lucinda's, 60th birthday next Thursday, and I was wondering if you could see your way to let us have a surprise party here. Nothing too fancy or expensive. A buffet would be fine'.

Dicky stroked his little goatee, hummed a bit, and said, 'How many would you like me to cater for?'

Roberto shrugged. 'Gee, I hadn't thought about it. I just expected a free-for-all open house'.

Dicky tittered and laughed. 'Roberto, there's no way Lucinda would like a load of unwashed trailer trash at her birthday bash. Why don't we make a short list of whom we know she likes, or at least tolerates?'

Dicky pulled out his pad and expensive fountain pen and said, 'Let's start with Cassy and Jimmy, Jeff, Gabby, Willie and Nobby—oh, and Elvira. Lucinda gets on well with Elvira. They're both potty on pussies'.

Roberto thought, *They're not the only ones.*

Roberto said, 'OK, but I'm not sure about Javier. He tends to get on Nobby's tits, always fussing over Willie, and I'm not sure how Lucinda would react if Javier turned up in some designer dress that outshined hers'.

Dicky said, 'Not to worry. Javier is doing his 7pm pantomime on Thursday evening at the town hall.' Dicky clapped his hands together. 'Just leave it up to me, Roberto. I'll do you a buffet to be proud of'.

'It won't be too flashy or expensive, will it?'

Dicky scribbled a few figures on his pad, looked up, and said, 'Fifty euro should do it, as long as people are buying at the bar. That will do me'.

Roberto breathed a sigh of relief, thanked Dicky, and said, 'You won't let it slip to Lucinda. Let's keep it a secret'.

Dicky said, 'Don't worry, Roberto, I'll discreetly inform the others about being here at 6.30pm on Thursday. This will give thirty minutes to get organised before you and Lucinda arrive at 7pm'.

Dicky wondered how he was going to tell his regulars he would be hosting a private bash, without them being invited. He would have to offer a 5 per cent discount for Friday, with the first drink free. That should keep the riffraff happy.

THURSDAY FINALLY CAME around. Dicky arrived at the bistro earlier than usual. He wanted to make sure his chef, Pierre, had remembered to go easy on the spice in the prawn cocktail. He was only thinking about Nobby's delicate institution, and the restaurant only had one gent's loo.

Nobby was fussing and fretting over the cake he was making for Lucinda's birthday. He just couldn't decide whether to use pink or green icing. *Pink it is. It'll match Lucinda's complexion after a tipple or two. Then again, she'll be green with envy if Javier turns up wearing his Vera Wang.*

Willie was strutting up and down in the bedroom, trying on his entire wardrobe, which was quite vast, nearly filling the whole second boudoir. *Do I go formal or flash? Decisions, decisions ... Lucinda would like flash, so my gold lamé pants and matching waistcoat it is*, he thought.

*

Two trailers down, Elvira was having the same problem. Thinking, *If I want to impress Dicky but not look too tarty, it's either my silver leggings and black boob tube, or my tiger-skin catsuit, meow.*

*

Roberto had taken Lucinda her morning coffee outside on the decking, his hands shaking so much that he spilt the coffee down his silk shirt. He was a bit worried about tonight and didn't want anything to go belly up.

Lucinda looked up and said, 'You're looking a little pale. You feeling OK? And why have I only got half a cup of coffee? Saving money on hot water are we?'

Roberto sat with a thud. 'I'm fine, just a little tired, that's all'.

Lucinda frowned. 'We can always have a rain check on our candlelit supper tonight. I'm sure Dicky won't mind'.

Roberto went bright red. 'How did you know we're going to Dicky's?'

Lucinda laughed. 'I know you well, Roberto. You're not one to splash your money about, and Dicky's is cheap'.

Roberto retorted, 'I'm not a tight arse. We're definitely going. I'll make you eat your words tonight for that quip'.

*

Cassy wondered if her mobility scooter would fit through Dicky's restaurant door. She could always leave it outside. *I'm sure I can manage from the door to the table.* But would it be safe outside? It was quite a dodgy area. *Never mind if it gets stolen. I know Jimmy will replace it with a better version. Problem solved.*

Jimmy was a little worried about the party tonight. He hoped with all his heart that no one had invited Kelly. He was racking his brain to remember whether Lucinda had met her. Cassie missed nothing, and if Kelly was there, he was sure she wouldn't resist nipping his derriere. His life wouldn't be worth living. Cassy was a Scorpio, with a hell of a sting in her tail.

*

Jeff was looking out his window, wondering why Dolly was later than usual. *I wonder if I should ask her to the party tonight. I know Lucinda won't mind.* She was usually friendly with Jeff.

But on second thought, you don't take coals to Newcastle, as the saying goes. What if there were lots of nubile ladies there?

*

Next door to Jeff, Gabby was putting wrapping paper on the cat mug she bought Lucinda. She knew Lucinda was mad about pussies. *So is Jeff,* she thought, *but not the four paws kind.*

'I know we were told not to bring presents', she said to herself, 'but Lucinda has always been kind to me. It's only a mug'.

12

SURPRISE PARTY TIME!

Dicky's bistro was situated next door to the clubhouse bar. It was small but done out tastefully. Fishing nets adorned the walls, oil lamps on every table—it all looked very nautical.

Dicky had made a real effort to hang fairy lights everywhere inside and out. He'd hung a Private Party, Invited Quests Only sign on the door. As soon as you entered you were greeted with a huge banner saying Happy 60th Birthday, Lucinda!

Dicky wasn't sure how Lucinda would feel about her age broadcast for all and sundry to see. What the hell, everyone coming knew her age anyway.

He had placed all the tables together in one long line in the middle of the room. He didn't want individual groups of four. That would lead to disaster, everyone squabbling about who sits with whom. Dicky did a last-minute check in the kitchen to make sure the buffet food was ready. Pierre had done him proud. There was a colourful array of vol-au-vents filled with various savoury ingredients, toads in the hole, and chicken fricassee.

'I just hope Lucinda appreciates the trouble, and this no-expense-spared party we have organised for her', he said to himself.

The guests were told to arrive at 6.45pm prompt. This way they would be here ready to shout surprise! when Roberto and Lucinda turned up at seven. Boy was she in for a shock, expecting a romantic candlelit supper for two.

The first to enter the bistro was Jimmy, with a puffing and wheezing Cassy leaning heavily on his arm. Cassy had parked her mobility scooter as near to the door as possible. She didn't want to tire herself out walking too far, and be damned if she was going to use her stick, thus avoiding being ridiculed.

Jimmy said to Dicky, 'Sorry we're a bit early'—it was 6.30pm— 'but Cassy needed first dibs on bagging a comfy seat'.

Dicky smiled, thinking, *With all her padding, she wouldn't notice if she was sat on a cactus.* 'I can't offer you a drink. We have to wait for the others before we open the cava. Although there is some leftover sangria in the fridge. Just help yourself'.

Cassy sat her huge bulk in the love seat under the window and shuffled about a bit until she felt comfy.

'Jimmy, go get me that sangria. It would be a shame to let it go to waste'.

Jimmy shot off behind the bar. Whilst he was pouring Cassy a generous portion into a goldfish-bowl-sized glass, he spied a can of Bud hidden behind the tonics. Quick as a flash he shoved it in his jacket pocket. He'd drink that as soon as he'd sat down.

Jimmy was slightly worried that if Cassy downed the whole glass before the others arrived, she'd be well on her way to being plastered before the night was through. How the hell would he get her home? The scooter wasn't big enough to do tandem.

The bistro door tinkled open as Cassy was just draining the last dregs of the glass. 'Oh goody', she said, 'bubbly time at last'.

Bursting through the door and making a lot of noise came the motley crew of guests. Jeff was rather loudly complimenting Willie on his light-up gold bowtie and matching trousers when Nobby pushed Willie inside, a little too roughly, sending Willie flying into the pampas plant (thank goodness it was plastic).

'Nobby, you prick' Willie said, going red in the face whilst trying to adjust his braces. 'Why did you push me?'

Nobby abruptly retorted, 'We would have been stood in the doorway until Lucinda's next birthday whilst you regurgitate where you bought your outfit, how much it cost, even down to what thong you are wearing'.

Jeff coughed and spluttered trying not to laugh. He made a beeline for the bar and started fiddling with the belt of his trousers. He thought he'd better let it out a notch or two, it was a tad tight, and if he wanted to do the buffet justice, he needed more belly room.

Gabby breezed in next, smelling like a mixture of lavender and stale sweat. She had managed to squeeze her robust figure into her pink evening gown, the one with the side split. Little did she know when she walked across the room, she was revealing a lot of lily-white thigh complete with cellulite. Her ample bosom was laden with a heavy set of pearls (not real), done on purpose to stop her heavy breasts swaying like pendulums when she got up to dance.

Willie was admiring Gabby's dress, which sparkled when she moved, but he didn't think her spandex would hold up under such stress. *Let's hope it lasts the night,* he said to himself. Willie shook his head, trying to get rid of an image of a huge, pink wobbling jelly.

Elvira was the last to enter, sashaying in. She wanted to make a grand entrance, let Dicky get an eyeful of her voluptuous curves. She'd poured herself into her tiger-skin catsuit. Her bosom yearned to be free. She'd made a mental note: remember not to bend down, even if she dropped her vol-au-vent, or out they would flop out like two eager puppies.

Elvira glided over to Dicky at the bar, batted her eyelashes, and said in a guttural voice, 'Meow'. Elvira had slugged back two vodkas on the rocks before leaving to give her Dutch courage to flirt with Dicky.

Dicky was a little flustered, turning a nice shade of pink. He wasn't used to women doing the chasing or being so forward.

Although he thought, *I quite like it—this evening could end up with horizontal refreshments for Elvira and me.*

Cassy shouted, 'Be quiet, everyone! Roberto and Lucinda are approaching'.

Dicky had ushered everyone away from the window, except Cassy who just ducked down, and told them to be ready to shout out surprise.

Roberto was talking very loudly to Lucinda, hoping the quests inside would hear him and hide in readiness.

Lucinda said, 'Why are you shouting, Roberto? I'm not deaf. I agree the bistro does look lovely all lit up like a Christmas tree. Can't remember it looking so festive before'.

Roberto gingerly opened the bistro door, silently praying Lucinda was in a good mood for socialising.

The first thing Lucinda clapped eyes on was the huge banner bearing her name in big letters, with her age shown for the whole world to see.

'I'll kill Roberto for this', she muttered. 'How dare he?'

Before she had time to berate him, a chorus of happy birthdays came echoing out of nowhere.

All at once she was bombarded with people saying how lovely she looked and how she didn't look her age.

Lucinda looked like the cat that got the cream, and she thanked them and turned to Roberto with a sickly smirk. 'Why didn't you tell me? I would have made an effort to get properly dressed for the occasion, instead of my humble attire'.

Lucinda was wearing an expensive designer Vera Wang trouser suit, black silk with a red sparkly boob tube. Luckily she had rinsed her hair with a silver grey tint, which complemented her outfit perfectly.

Roberto had sidled off to the bar whilst the fussing was going on. 'Dicky' he said, 'give me a large whisky sour. I need it desperately, Lucinda has spent all day tarting herself up, fussing over what accessories to wear, make-up and whatnot. If I didn't know better, I'd say she knew about tonight.'

Dicky said, 'Thank goodness we men don't have to bother, unless you're Javier, that is'. Dicky rang the bell. 'Ladies and germs, I now declare the bar is open'.

Six bottles of Cava had been popped open in quick succession. Nobby, Roberto, Jeff, and Jimmy thought Cava was a tart's drink so opted for the Bud. Roberto paid for the beers.

Dicky whispered to Roberto, 'The Cava is gratis, but any more and you'll have to dig deep in your pocket'.

Elvira volunteered to help Dicky uncover the buffet food, finding any excuse to rub against him.

The booze was flowing, food was diminishing rapidly, and all you could hear was the incessant chatter and raucous laughter mingling with the background music.

Willie jumped up and headed for the antiquated jukebox in the corner because the records were free. This relic was Dicky's pride and joy, given to him on his 50th birthday by Rocky, who owned the antiques shop on the high street.

Sadly, Rocky had died of a heart attack last year. The jukebox was one of Dicky's treasured possessions. Both he and his clientele had enjoyed years of listening to his prize collection of 50s, 60s, 70s and 80s records.

Willie selected Tina Turner's "Private Dancer", threw his jacket off, and started gyrating behind Nobby's chair.

Not to miss an opportunity, Elvira jumped up grabbed hold of Dicky and danced round him seductively, everything moving in the right direction.

Jimmy didn't know where to look. Every time he tried to focus on Cassy and her droning voice, his eyes would betray him and automatically turn to Elvira's bumping and grinding.

Cassy gave Jimmy a swift kick under the table for looking at Elvira while licking his lips. Elvira was nothing short of a prick teaser.

Jimmy had no chance, Cassy thought. *He couldn't cope with me, and I'm a nighty-on, lights-on kind of person, not a bit demanding, take it or leave it, and Jimmy prefers to leave it. How we managed to have two kids is still a mystery. I'm sure Jimmy was more virile in his youth. Perhaps he's got erectile dysfunction and is too ashamed to talk about it.*

Gabby decided she didn't want to be left out so asked Jeff if he would like to dance. Jeff slyly looked around, decided he wasn't going to get a better deal, and smiled and said, 'Let's go shake a leg, Gabby.'

Roberto had ushered Lucinda out on the dance floor. They were doing a slow smooch, cheek to cheek. Roberto liked to keep his passionate side to himself, in his own home. He knew Lucinda was a bit of a cold fish and didn't like to give the impression that she might actually enjoy intimacy.

Lucinda was secretly thinking, *Why can't Roberto be more spontaneous like Willie, who was now giving his all?* Even Nobby had relentlessly given in and was doing a version of a *Saturday Night Fever* dance.

The bistro was reeling and rocking, looking like something out of *The Last Tango in Paris*, hot and steamy windows. The door opened slowly and in popped Javier, who was totally gob smacked.

Javier couldn't remember if he had been invited, and totally forgot—or had they thought he would be performing at the town hall? What luck the generator had packed in and would take a couple of days to fix.

What a coincidence he had bumped into Lena and Harry, who were on their way to the chippy, when they all heard the commotion coming from the bistro. They couldn't resist peeking in through the steamy window and saw a sight for sore eyes. All of his neighbours were cavorting and gyrating all over the place.

The temptation was too much for them to ignore, so Javier opened the door wide and ushered Lena and Harry inside. The door closed with a tinkle, but no one seemed to notice.

Willie missed his footing whilst trying to be too acrobatic and fell back, straight into Javier's arms.

Nobby looked like he was about to blow a fuse and said, 'I should have known you would have made sure Javier was invited, so you could flirt quite openly, Willie'.

Javier gently eased Willie to his wobbly feet and said with a smile, 'Thanks for the invite, Willie'.

Willie spluttered, going redder and redder in the face, and every time he tried to speak his tongue refused to work. He could only open and shut his mouth like a fish.

Nobby picked up his glass of beer and flung it straight at Javier, who ducked, and it hit Lena full in the face. Harry went to punch Nobby, but Dicky stuck his foot out and Harry fell head first into Cassy's lap. Luckily for Cassy her padding saved her from any bruising or pain.

Jimmy jumped up and helped Harry to his feet, stuttering, 'I didn't know you and Lena were invited'.

Lena was busy trying to wipe beer foam off her face, using her kaftan as a towel, showing off her blue Bridget Jones's to perfection.

Nobby was apologising profusely, trying to mop up the beer off her boobs with his handkerchief.

Harry, now on his feet, noticed the button on his pants had popped off and his flies were down, revealing his spotted jockstrap, showing a rather large bulge—every time his adrenaline kicked in, he got a hard-on.

Javier had sidled over to Roberto and Lucinda, who were staring goggle eyed at the rumpus. Lucinda noticed Javier next to her and gave an inward scream. Javier was wearing a Louis Vuitton special edition three-piece outfit with Jimmy Choo pixie boots.

How dare he try to outshine her at her own birthday party?

Javier looked Lucinda up and down, smiled, and said, 'How gauche to wear a Vera Wang twinned with a top shop boob tube'. *Shame she doesn't have much to put in it,* he thought. Lucinda was quite flat chested, looked like an ironing board.

Javier thought, *Serves her right for being a stuck-up cow and not inviting me, although I do like her trouser suit. It would look better on me though.*

Javier shot off quickly to sit with Cassy, who would protect him. No one tackled Cassy. She had a left hook that Muhammad Ali would be proud of.

Lucinda stood with her mouth wide open, looking like she was catching flies or ready to cry.

Roberto cringed. How had this happened? He quickly grabbed Lucinda, sat her down, and gave her a large glass of Cava. 'Drink it down in one gulp, Lucinda', he said. 'It'll make you feel better.'

Lucinda knocked it back in one go. 'I'll show that tranny a thing or two', she said. 'Roberto, I want you to physically throw him out, and make sure he lands in a puddle of mud, ruining his clothes. And get rid of Flash Harry and Lena at the same time. Tell them their gate crashing is not welcome, or my party will be totally ruined, and I'll blame you for a long time'.

Roberto shot off to the gents, letting Lucinda calm down, plying her with more bubbly. He thought he was no match for beefy Harry or Lena—they would make mincemeat out of him.

Elvira was slumped in Dicky's arms, totally oblivious to the chaos around her. Dicky was struggling to keep her upright, and he gave one massive heave ho under her arms. Down went Elvira's top, releasing her enormous boobs.

Dicky's eyes nearly popped out of his head. If he let go to pull up her top, she would slump to the floor, giving everyone an eyeful. Dicky held Elvira even closer so no one could see her front, and gestured to Jimmy, who seemed the only one in charge of his senses, to come over, mouthing, 'I need your help'.

Jimmy manoeuvred himself round all the gyrating and fighting going on, over to Dicky. He nearly fainted when he got an eyeful of Elvira's torpedoes. *Jeez*, he thought. *Cassy's are big but these are bazookas.*

Dicky and Jimmy managed to get Elvira's top back in place and half dragged her over to the chaise lounge, flipping her down none too gently.

*

Lena finally wiped her face. Her mascara was running down her cheeks, her lipstick smeared all over. She lunged towards the bar and slumped her heavy bulk on the stool, which nearly disappeared. Lena shouted to Harry, 'Get me a large glass of vino, and a plate of food before I faint of hunger'.

Harry had quickly zipped up his flies and didn't give a toss who'd had an eyeful. They'd only be jealous of his Rolls-Royce, not a mini like Nobby's the skinny Mary Ellen. He swayed over to Lena, shouting over to Dicky to do his duty and serve them quickly if he valued having two balls.

Dicky sighed. *What a night!* he thought. *Elvira's out cold, no chance of my happy ending there then.* Everyone was drunk, and tempers were hotting up.

Lucinda was shouting rather loudly for Roberto, who was nowhere to be seen. She was desperately trying to keep it together and act like a lady, which was becoming extremely difficult seeing she was pie-eyed. What the hell, every lady was entitled to a day off.

Cassy was knocking back the vino like it was water, shouting for Willie to come over and sit with her because Jimmy was too occupied with making sure Elvira was still breathing.

Cassy whispered to Willie, 'Revenge is a dish best served cold. Just wait until Jimmy puts on his undercrackers—complete with Fiery Jack ointment'.

Cassy and Willie were giggling uncontrollably when Nobby stormed over.

Nobby, red in the face, retorted, 'Oh, so you find this fiasco amusing do you? Everyone showing themselves up, especially you, Willie'.

Willie giggled again, tried to speak, but his words just came out a mumbled mess.

Cassy gave Nobby a cold stare. 'Just lighten up, chill out, let your hair down, get rat arsed like the rest of us'.

Willie started giggling again and stuttered, 'Nobby doesn't have any hair, Cassy—only where the sun don't shine'.

Nobby stormed off in disgust and headed for the bar to talk to Dicky, who was the only sane one here, beside himself, of course.

Harry saw Nobby making a beeline towards the bar, so he picked up one of Lena's vol-au-vents and flung it straight at Nobby—a perfect hit—straight in the smacker.

Nobby gasped and hid behind the bar. He picked up the soda syphon and squirted it straight at Harry, plastering his greasy hair flatly to his head.

Dicky was trying unsuccessfully to wrestle the syphon out of Nobby's hands, and Lena was in hysterics, nearly falling off her buffet.

Roberto had just vacated the gents and went flying on his back, skidding and sliding on beer and soggy bits of food. He barged straight into Jeff's chair, sending Gabby—who happened to be sitting on Jeff's knee—toppling on to Roberto, Gabby was laughing hysterically.

Jeff was trying to untangle them both whilst trying not to laugh out loud. Roberto must have been winded and bruised—Gabby was a big lady.

Lucinda had witness the whole scene and tried to stand up, to give Roberto a piece of her mind for showing her up like a drunken thug. But Lucinda's legs refused to obey, and she slumped back down, grabbing the table edge as she went, which toppled over, glasses and plates smashing to the floor. Everyone stared at her just lying there.

Lucinda groaned. *This is Roberto's fault!* she thought. *I've never been so humiliated. I think I'm going to cry.*

Jimmy came to Lucinda's rescue, whipping her up off the floor, dusting her down with a serviette, trying to soothe her hurt pride while she blubbered loudly on his shoulder. *I hope Cassy doesn't see this, I'll never hear the ending,* he thought.

*

Next door in the clubhouse, Pedro was downing his eighth pint. His mate, Julio, was struggling with his seventh. They had a 10.00 euro bet on who could down ten pints first, and he was winning, hands down. He was just embarking on his ninth pint when the painting of the campsite hanging on the wall came crashing down. The wall was fairly shaking.

'What the hell is going on next door at the bistro?' he said. He could hear a hell of a commotion going on, mixed with blaring music.

Pedro said to Julio, 'Get the fuzz down here fast. Tell them the bistro is breaking the camp rules, upsetting the rest of the residents'—which Pedro didn't actually give a toss about—'and Dicky needs a warning'.

Pedro was more interested in wiping the floor with Dicky. He'd love to close him down, seeing Pedro was banned from eating in there.

Pedro barged out of the clubhouse, staggered next door to the bistro, and slammed the door open, nearly taking it off its hinges.

The sight that met his eyes beggared belief. Typical trailer trash. They were all trashed, and the bistro looked like a bomb site.

'What the hell is going on? Dicky's ruining my chance of winning a 10.00 euro bet. I'll make you pay for this.' Pedro picked Dicky up by the throat with one hand and pinned him up against the wall.

Dicky was spluttering and going a nice shade of pink in the face.

No one noticed Elvira staggering over, one boob swaying loosely. She headed straight for Pedro and kicked him right between the legs from behind. 'Goal!' she shouted. 'I've wanted to do that for years'.

Pedro dropped Dicky like a hot potato, fell to the floor clutching his wedding tackle, shouting for ice.

Roberto shot over to the ice bucket and chucked it over Pedro's throbbing private parts.

Jeff was shouting to everyone that they should all scamper pretty quickly before Pedro had time to recover. He would make their lives hell from now on.

Everyone was squabbling and talking loudly, the drunk leading the drunk, when an ear-splitting whistle came from the doorway. In charged three *official de policia*, truncheons at the ready. No one messes with the Spanish Gendarmerie.

Elvira said in a slurred voice, 'Hola, occifers! Arrest that gypsy, he tried to rape me—look!' She thrust her loose boob at them. 'He also tried to kill my Dicky!'

Dicky blushed and pulled Elvira away, scooping up her top at the same time.

Everyone was trying very loudly to talk at once. Oficial Perry blew his whistle again. 'Quiet! You're all coming down to the station. Perhaps a night in a cell to sober up might make you more cooperative in the morning'.

*

The sun came streaming into the cell at 6.30am. Willie, Nobby, Jeff, and Dicky could be heard snoring in their bunkbeds.

Dicky woke up first, knowing instantly where he was. He unfortunately had been sober last night, when they were locked up. He shook Jeff awake.

Jeff opened one eye, groaned, and said, 'What you doing in my bedroom, Dicky?'

Dicky shook him again. 'We're in frigging jail, you idiot. Can't you remember?'

Nobby heard Dicky's loud voice. 'How did we get into this awful ordeal? I blame Javier, Dicky'.

Willie kept his eyes shut. He didn't want them to know he'd been awake for a while, feeling sorry for himself. He just wished he could remember what had happened for them to end up locked up.

Did Nobby murder Javier? He groaned and turned over.

Next cell down, Lucinda was in the top bunk, and Roberto in the bottom bunk. Lucinda was at it hammer and tongs at Roberto, who had only slept for a few hours, whereas Lucinda had been out like a light and only woke when she'd heard Nobby shouting next door.

Lucinda's viscous tongue was firing obscenities at Roberto, blaming him for her having to end up in a smelly, damp cell. Her designer clothes would have to be thrown away—she'd never be able to get rid of the smell. She would make sure Roberto replaced every last item, right down to her underwear.

Roberto was taking it on the chin, staying calm, not wanting to retaliate and give Lucinda more ammunition.

In the cell opposite theirs, Elvira and Gabby were snoring in unison, oblivious to their surroundings, Elvira dreaming of being in a clinch with Dicky. Gabby had images of she and Jeff going at it like rabbits on heat.

Further down the corridor were two single cells. One held Pedro, because they didn't want to risk putting him with anyone else. They knew Pedro from old—his temper got him into lots of trouble—he was a hot-headed thug who used his fists first.

In the other single cell, Javier was pacing up and down, wondering if everyone else was on their own or just him because he was different.

Javier was right. Did they put him with the men or women? Much safer to put him on his own.

Harry and Lena had not been taken to jail. Lena had been rushed to hospital because she fell off her buffet and cracked her head. They had to make sure she hadn't a concussion. Luckily, because she had been inebriated, she'd fallen like a rag doll, so no brain damage, but they wanted to keep her overnight just as a precaution.

Harry had been allowed to go with her, and he stayed until morning, sleeping in the chair next to her bed.

They had both been told to report to the Policia Municipal as soon as possible to give statements.

Cassy too was spared the indignation of spending the night in the cells, due to her disability, needing a scooter. Jimmy had been allowed to be escorted home with her because he told them he was her carer and had to help her go to the toilet (which was a total fabrication). Cassy was quite capable of doing these things herself but wanted to milk it while she could.

Inspector Jefe had asked one of his colleagues to attend their trailer and take statements as soon as possible. He also asked Official Jenny to interview all the ladies individually. He said he would interview the men. And Javier.

Dicky was first to be dealt with because he was the proprietor of the bistro. Dicky gave his side of the story, not hyping anything up or twisting the facts.

Jeff followed next, followed in quick succession by Nobby and Willie, all telling roughly the same distorted version.

Roberto was grateful when it came to his turn, giving him the excuse to get away from Lucinda.

He asked Inspector Jefe to be gentle with Lucinda, telling him it wasn't her fault things went belly up. Her birthday had been ruined, and she would never forget that.

Inspector Jefe sent for Javier, who came in huffing and puffing, demanding to know why he had been arrested—didn't they know he was an artist and not to be tarred by the same brush as the other riffraff?

Inspector Jefe wanted to let Pedro stew in his cell until late afternoon, in the hope he would calm down. This was not the first time, they'd had run-ins with Pedro.

By late afternoon Inspector Jefe and Official Jenny had obtained everyone's statements, accusations flying everywhere. They both came to the same conclusion. This was a birthday party that had got out of hand and turned into a bun fight free-for-all due to too much consumption of alcohol, petty jealousies, and clashing of personalities. A bigger set of misfits Jefe had yet to find.

What a waste of policia time, not to mention free board and lodgings at their expense. He'd a good mind to charge them. Instead, he'd told them they had to rectify the damage done to Dicky's bistro, either by money or helping out at the bistro.

The only consolation was that they would think twice about partying again. And this would test their mettle.

Would they be able to move on and not hold grudges against each other? They had all shown their true colours in person, remaining friends would yet to be seen.

Pedro was going to be a different kettle of fish. He would be given a stiff fine and threatened with deportation if he tried to seek retaliation of any kind. Plus, Jefe was going to contact the owner of the trailer park and ask that Pedro be relocated to another trailer park, preferably in Australia.

He was going to pay a call to Dicky's bistro in a couple of days, just to make sure everything was sorted. He would also leave a charity jar at the bar for the policia ball and make sure they contributed out of sheer shame.

13

LIFE GOES ON (for some).

Lucinda woke with a brass band playing in her head. Self-inflicted, due to the excessive consumption of Cava and Brandy she'd wolfed down since her disastrous party night, hoping to dull her senses so she wouldn't have to dwell on the degradation of spending a night in a Spanish jail.

Trust Roberto to make a hash of it, she thought. Lucinda would have been quite happy spending the evening just the two of them, at an exclusive tapas bar, and maybe a surprise present. A Mediterranean cruise would have been nice, even some expensive jewellery.

What Roberto spent on a free-for-all bun fight sham of a party, they probably could have afforded both.

Lucinda crawled out of bed groaning and headed straight for the medicine cabinet in the bathroom. Out came the paracetamols, which she would wash down with a large glass of bloody Mary. That should do the trick.

'I just wish I could beam myself to outer Mongolia' she said. 'For a whole year'.

I'll never live this down, she thought. *The embarrassment would be too much to bear.* What if Joyce heard about her spending the night in a cell? *Oh, I'll never be able to show my face again at the spa. No more massages from Enzo!*

She was wondering where the hell Roberto was. *We shall be having a serious talk when he decides to show up with his tail between his legs. I want to move far away,* she thought.

*

Roberto had been up early to go for a jog on the front to clear his mind. He was at a loss as to what peace offering he could give Lucinda, apart from his head on a plate.

His mobile rang, and he groaned loudly. *I hope it's not Lucinda,* he thought. He answered on the third ring.

'Hola', a doddering female voice said, 'am I speaking to Roberto?'

'Yes, who is it?'

'My name's Irene. I live next door to your mum, Giselle. I'm sorry to tell you she's just been taken by ambulance to Lavanty Hospital. Giselle had a bad fall, and they are worried about concussion. She wanted me to let you know'.

Roberto sighed heavily. 'Thank you, Irene. I'll go to the hospital straightaway'.

Roberto didn't want to go back to the trailer to change, Lucinda would be on the warpath, and he could do without more stress. Luckily he always carried his bum bag round his waist, just in case he needed refreshing.

So he ran round the Rincon to the taxi rank, jumped in, and said to the driver, 'Take me to Lavanty Hospital, por favour'.

His mind was all over the place. Would his mum be OK? If not, who would look after her? He was an only child; no way would Lucinda allow him to become her care nurse.

Roberto thought he had better check on his mum's villa, make sure she hadn't left the gas on. He would have Dicky give him a lift to Villa joyosa Village, where it was situated.

*

Harry was taking Yellow for his daily walk. He'd left Lena snoring like a pig. It was so quiet early morning; not many people about to disturb his solitude.

He was going to swing by the office on his way back and pick up the mail. He was in no mood to see Pedro. Harry was definitely a match for Pedro—he had at least two stone on him.

Yellow was barking his head off just outside Elvira's. He'd spotted Ginger in the window, one of Elvira's mangy moggies.

'Shut the hell up, Yellow. I don't want Elvira on my back. Her bite's worse than her bark—just ask Pedro'. *Although I wouldn't mind Elvira coming out in her see-through nightie. She's very tasty,* he thought.

Harry was so engrossed in his daydreams, he hadn't noticed Yellow had done his jobs and he stepped right onto it, squishing all over his Jesus sandals, squelching through his toes. 'Shit, Yellow, you effing mutt!' Harry had never bothered taking a pooper scooper out with him because poop was biodegradable and good for the environment.

Harry cursed loudly. He would have to return home to get cleaned up. *Let's hope Lena is still asleep, otherwise she'll want me to cook her breakfast and fetch her fags. What did her last slave die of?* he thought.

Harry squelched back up to his trailer, dragging a whiny Yellow behind him.

Lena was bustling about in her kitchen, not sure what she fancied this morning for breakfast. She said to herself, 'Harry usually makes it for me, but the lazy bugger is nowhere to be seen. I'll make Welsh rarebit with four rashes of bacon on the side. Harry can get his own breakfast. He'll be gone most off the morning anyway. He usually calls in at Benito's Cafe for his morning espresso. Benito always has a bowl of something for Yellow, so that'll be nice'.

Lena had just squeezed her bulk into the dining chair and squirted tomato sauce all over her food when the door burst open. Harry came storming in, shouting swear words directed at Yellow that a lady shouldn't have to hear.

'What the hell is that smell, Harry?'

He lifted his foot up, which was dripping brown poop.

Lena yelled, 'Get outside, you dirty bastard and go wash your feet with the hose pipe! I was really looking forward to my breakfast, and now I feel like barfing'.

Lena shouted after Harry as he inched out the door, 'You'd better hose down Yellow too. Nether of you come back in until I inspect you both'.

Harry couldn't believe anything would come between Lena and her grub; this was a first.

Lena went outside and asked Harry, 'Did Pedro give you any grief about the party? I hope you told him we were all having fun until he spoilt it'.

Harry laughed. 'Yeah, it was fun. I love a good scrap, and it was worth it just to see the look on Lucinda's stuck-up face'.

*

Nobby was absorbed in his computer, looking at Nordic cruises. He was really interested in seeing the Northern

Lights (Aurora Borealis) and Iceland. He desperately needed to get himself and Willie away for a long spell, and somewhere cold would be ideal to cool down Willies anger.

Maybe go for a couple of months, until the dust dies down, giving everyone time to forget their terrible ordeal. What luck—the *Oceanic Queen* was sailing next weekend. A few cabins and suites were still available. He decided a suite it would be; he could afford it. Willie would be impressed when he saw the sheer luxury of their private boudoir, on the top deck with spectacular views.

Nobby grabbed his wallet, whipped out his gold card, and booked it there and then. He would surprise Willie when they were having their evening meal.

Here's hoping, he thought, *that this good news would make Willie crack a smile.* He hadn't seen him smile since the party. Willie just moped about with a dazed look on his face.

Nobby decided to get better insurance coverage, just in case. Nobby had already experienced a mild heart attack, so he wanted to be sure Willie would be fine financially if God forbid anything did happen to him or Willie.

*

Willie was trying to watch his favourite programme, *Horrible Histories*, but his mind kept wandering off. He was finding it difficult to concentrate on the rotten Romans.

Would he ever be able to show his face in public again? He just couldn't remember much about how the party ended in such a fiasco. It was like seeing a jigsaw with missing pieces.

Willie had not gone out since the party, which was six nights ago. He daren't sneak across to Cassy's to get the whole story; he was too worried what Nobby would think.

Willie just had to take Nobby's word for it that it was all Javier's fault, and he kept rubbing it in that Willie had invited him, but his memory couldn't recall if he had or not.

He just wished Nobby would go out so he could sneak across to Cassy's. But Dicky's bistro was closed for repairs, so Nobby wouldn't be taking any fairy cakes to Dicky just yet.

Willie was glad all the party dwellers had coughed up and given Dicky 500 euros, plus Roberto, Jimmy, Jeff, and Nobby had offered to help with the repairs and DIY.

I could try to get Nobby to pick up my prescription from the local chemist for my allergies, he thought. That would give Willie at least an hour to sprint over to Cassie's.

*

Cassy was sitting in her usual position overlooking the promenade and the beach. She kept having a sneaky peek up towards Willie's trailer, hoping to catch him outside and get him to come over and have a coffee and catch up on gossip before it became yesterday's news.

She was worried about Willie. She knew what a control freak Nobby was; he'd probably got him chained to the bed. Cassy shuddered. *If only my legs would get me up there, I could make sure Willie was OK. Perhaps I could ask Jimmy to pop up on some pretence of borrowing a lemon for my G&T.*

Cassy suddenly had second thoughts. Jimmy was still smarting from the effects of the hot undercrackers he'd put on the day after the party. Cassie stifled a giggle. He looked so funny jumping around the place, scratching his private parts. She had felt sorry for him in the end so offered him some aloe vera to smother on his underused tackle.

Cassie told Jimmy it was probably the cheap washing powder he'd bought from the Smart Mart, telling him to get allergen-free in the future.

Cassy had noticed a change in Jimmy since the party. He was more subdued than normal and had this vacant look, like he was somewhere else. *He'd better not be thinking of Elvira or he'll get a double dose next time.*

*

Jimmy had just left Kelly in the coffee shop after having two espressos to give him the buzz he needed to get him through his working day. Since Lucinda's party, he'd had a rude wakeup call. He didn't want to spend the rest of his life being nursemaid to Cassy—not to mention being her slave. He couldn't remember the last time they'd been intimate; she just didn't turn him on anymore. Cassy was too bothered about her G&Ts and chitchats with Willie to be concerned about her appearance, or whether Jimmy was around.

I'm going to have a serious talk with Cassy, he thought. *I'll suggest we go to counselling, give her the chance to change. She could also go for elastic band in the stomach operation to get to eat less and lose weight. Also, there are local AA meetings to wean her off her gins.*

I suppose I owe it to Cassy to give her another chance. He had loved her at one point in his life, so maybe they could recapture that. Jimmy sighed, knowing he was grasping at straws. Only something short of a miracle would get Cassy to accept these terms.

It was perhaps time to take Kelly's advice and grow a pair, show her who's boss. After all, he had worked hard to bring home the bacon, trying to keep her in the style she was accustomed to—plenty of booze, food, and being a couch potato.

*

Jeff was waving goodbye to Dolly, his cleaning lady, when he glimpsed Gabby peeking through the curtains. She was probably jealous of his relationship with Dolly, especially after what happened at the party. Gabby was now under the impression that he and Gabby were now an item.

Jeff was still unsure how he felt about shacking up with Gabby. On the negative side, he'd have to let Dolly go, and he'd have to curb his roving eye. On the positive side, Gabby was comfortably off; her ex had left her with a tidy sum.

They could both sell their trailers and move into one of the over-60s bungalows in Meadow Pastures. He knew there were still a few available for rent. Dolly's parents, who were in their 80s, lived there, and they loved it. It had an indoor and outdoor pool, a classy club bar, restaurant, and tennis courts. They would be escaping this concentration camp, with psycho Pedro in charge.

Jeff didn't think he'd miss anyone at the campsite, although he did get on well with most of them—the exception being Harry and Lena, a couple of misfit weirdos if ever there were.

Jeff and Gabby could pool their pensions and have a good time eating out, taking holidays, even getting a dog. Great for exercise and making new friends with other dog walkers.

Perhaps the time had come for him to settle down. He knew Gabby would jump at the chance.

*

Gabby was having a secret peek behind her curtains, spying on Jeff waving Dolly off. She had mixed feelings about this; she didn't think Dolly was the least bit interested. She was too young, plus she had a new boyfriend in tow. Gabby had seen them coming out of Julio's tapas bar, holding hands and gazing into each other's eyes.

I think it's just wishful thinking on Jeff's part, she thought. *He knows he won't get past first base.* No. If he had any sense, Jeff would recognise what a catch Gabby was. She was a good cook, and he wouldn't want for anything, especially in the bedroom.

It was time to put plan B in operation—make him jealous, drop a few hints about Juan's little gifts he'd bought her, plus flowers. She'd also tell him how Juan was desperate to get her into bed (he already had) but she was holding out for the right man.

She decided to invite Jeff for a weekend away, take a break from all this toxic atmosphere. Her sister had a camper van, which was empty until next month, parked at Beavers Brook. They wouldn't need to take much, sleep in the buff. There was a lovely little Super Marche on the site where they could go to buy what they needed food-wise.

Gabby was getting all giddy and hot under the collar just thinking about it. She'd wait until dark and then head over to Jeff's. She didn't want anyone to see her. It would be their little secret.

*

Elvira was up early, feeding her entourage when she heard Yellow barking. She promptly removed Ginger, opened the window wide, and got ready to give Harry a piece of her mind. She was just in time to see him trying to shake off Yellow's stools. Elvira put her hand over her mouth to stifle a giggle. *Serves him right, the old goat,* she thought, *spoiling Lucinda's party.* Elvira couldn't remember much, but putting snippets together that Dicky had told her, everything was going great until they arrived with Javier in tow.

Shame they didn't spend the night in cells, but poor Lena had spent the night in hospital. She could have died, or worse, been cabbaged. Mind you, she wasn't much different now.

Harry and Lena were on a different planet than everyone else— "weirdos" didn't quite cover it.

Elvira hummed as she washed the mountain of cat dishes in the sink. She really felt she'd got past first base with Dicky; it was only a matter of time before she had him eating out her hands.

How could she instigate round two? She had better come up with a good plan, maybe offer him advice on some new decor for his bistro. Or make him one of her special casseroles and take it to the bistro tomorrow when he would be decorating during the day. They say the way to a man's heart is through his stomach, so here's hoping.

*

The bistro door was wide open, and Pedro's handyman, Juan, was fixing the loose hinges. Dicky was busy fussing over his books; luckily, Jefe's harsh words had worked wonders. The bistro looked better than ever. The walls had been painted, the floor stained, and everything smelled fresh and clean. This was down to Roberto, Jimmy, Jeff, Nobby, and Dicky. They had all worked hard to get the bistro up and running, ready for the weekend rush.

Dicky had been juggling figures and was satisfied everything was in order, ready for Gustave to peruse. Gustave owned the clubhouse next door and was always pestering Dicky to sell the bistro to him so he could knock through and make it one big bar/restaurant. Dicky had always refused. He'd been happy here. Not anymore though, after the fiasco at Lucinda's party. He'd had enough; he wasn't getting any younger, and it was time to sell and move on to something a little easier to manage.

He was hoping he could persuade Elvira to up sticks and join him, pussies included. He didn't think he'd have to work too hard on this decision after she'd made it pretty clear she fancied him. With the proceeds of the bistro and his trailer, he'd be comfortably off. They would just have to decide together where they would like to locate to, maybe a little cafe in the hustle of town and a small holding in the mountains, great for the moggies.

*

It was 9.05 and the office was still locked. A few residents had already tried the door, frustrated.

'How dare Pedro keep them waiting? Lazy git. He should have opened up five minutes ago', Gabby said.

She was in the queue, ready to give him a piece of her mind. She'd had a bellyful of his bullshit, and he needed to be put in his place.

The door finally opened fifteen minutes later by Juan, with no sign of Pedro. Juan apologised and said, 'I just received a text from Pedro asking me to open up'.

*

Pedro was lying in Sammy's bed (his ex). He'd arrived late last night at her trailer on the outskirts of Glen Valley. He'd knocked on her trailer and collapsed inside when she opened the door. Pedro laid it on thick, saying he had been attacked by the residents at his park. He told her such a sob story about how they had threatened him with violence if he didn't leave. He also told her the policia had got hold of his boss and told him a pack of lies about what happened the other night at Dicky's. They needed a scapegoat, and unfortunately, he was it. They had always had it in for him—his boss had sacked him, and he was worried the policia might try to extradite him.

Sammy had fallen for it hook, line, and sinker; she had no love for the gendarmes; they were just bullies. She took him into her bed to console him. They would talk about it in the morning.

Morning came, and Sammy came into the bedroom. She'd got up early to make Pedro a cup of tea, and when she entered the bedroom, he had his head in his hands, groaning.

Sammy was concerned and said, 'Are you hurt somewhere?'

Pedro smiled secretly, his plan working to perfection. 'Oh, Sammy, I'm so sorry we split up. We were good together, and I'm a changed man. I don't go binging with the boys anymore. I'm quite happy to watch TV or go for a long walk'.

Pedro looked up with a sad expression and said, 'We can we have another go at making it work. I do miss you. I've been saving really hard and have built up a little nest egg, so we can start afresh somewhere else where no one knows us'.

Pedro continued, 'I know of a trailer park in Estepona. The manager is retiring and is advertising for a replacement, preferably a married couple to run it together. Sammy, would you do me the honour of becoming my wife again please?'

Sammy looked surprised. 'I need to think about this. Give me some time to digest it, and in the meantime you can stay here. We'll try courting again, have date nights—what do you say, Pedro?'

Pedro's beaming smile said it all.

*

Javier was taking his Louis Vuitton trouser suit to the local cleaners due to it being terribly creased—not to mention a bit stinky. *What do you expect if you spend the night in a cell still wearing it eight hours after?* he thought, and he wasn't stupid enough to chuck it out, like Lucinda had done with her designer outfit, crazy bitch, more money than sense that one. She could have donated it to charity or even better, given it to him. One should never look a gift horse in the mouth.

Javier carried on towards the town hall. The generator had been repaired, thank goodness, so it was business as usual, the show must go on. He was looking forward to tonight's performance; acting came natural to him.

His mind wandered to thinking about Willie. He felt sorry for him, married to that tyrant, Nobby. Willie deserved better, someone like himself, for instance. He would treat him with the respect he deserved.

Javier said to himself, 'I must remember after the show to call in at Dicky's and apologise'.

After all, it was Nobby who had started it. Then those two idiots, Harry and Lena, just had to give their two pennies' worth, making Javier look bad, for letting them in. He would make sure in the future to give those two nutters a wide berth.

14

HASTA LA VISTA (goodbye)!

Lucinda and Robert were busily making for-sale signs, complete with contact details, to place in the trailer windows.

Lucinda was so excited; she couldn't wait to tell Pedro where he could stick his ground rent demands.

Lucinda hadn't had the chance to rant and rave about moving away because Roberto had burst in, shouting, 'Lucinda! Guess what? We're moving'.

Roberto spent more than an hour in the hospital, fussing and fretting about his mum. He was relieved to hear she had cuts, bruises, and a sprained ankle, but nothing majorly serious. The doctor had explained that his mum was too frail and forgetful to live independently and would need a full-time carer.

Roberto sighed and said he couldn't take on that responsibility because he worked full time, and there wasn't a cat in hell's chance Lucinda would contemplate it.

The doctor told Roberto to go to the front desk and the receptionist would give him a list of good nursing homes that had availability. In the meantime, his mum would remain in hospital until a place was booked.

Roberto had managed to have a long talk with his mum, telling her she would have to sell her villa and move into a home because they would need the money to finance the nursing home.

Giselle had smiled at Roberto, and in a frail voice said that wouldn't be necessary, she had been preparing for this day so everything was taken care of. The villa was in his name. She had transferred it over to him five years ago as a gift. 'I have some savings put aside for a rainy day, and it happens to be raining now. Because I've been a Spanish citizen resident for more than twenty years, I get my nursing home fees paid for. Therefore, my savings and pension will give me a comfortable life'.

Roberto left the hospital in a daze. He couldn't believe his luck—he was now the proud owner of a two-bed, mortgage-free bungalow with a neat garden and a communal pool. *Wait until Lucinda hears this—if this news doesn't make her icy heart melt, nothing will.*

Lucinda had wasted no time in visiting the bungalow, measuring up for curtains, deciding what furniture to keep or get rid of.

Roberto and Lucinda had organised a moving date for the weekend coming.

Roberto said to Lucinda, 'Why don't we have a farewell party at Dicky's on Friday night to say goodbye properly?'

He just managed to duck as a wet dishcloth was flung straight at him. *I guess that was Lucinda's final word.*

*

Harry came back from the office clutching a rather official-looking letter. As soon as he got back to his trailer, he ripped the envelope open and couldn't believe what it said.

He'd forgotten about him and Lena having their names down on the waiting list for sheltered housing in Bunny Meadows. He had done it because he was worried about Lena's health going downhill. She was getting more and more forgetful, leaving things on the stove too long, leaving the tap on in the bathroom. He couldn't watch her all the time; he wasn't getting any younger either.

The letter informed him a vacancy of a one bed was available, would he like to view it on Tuesday? It was now Saturday. The financial costs were far less than what they paid here. Pedro was draining them dry.

Harry shouted for Lena to come quickly and read this letter.

Lena groaned. 'Not another bill from dick face, I hope'. She snatched the letter, and her eyes nearly popped out of her head.

93

'Harry, this is great! Just what we need—a fresh start, not to mention how well we'll be looked after. They have communication cords and coms, so if you need anything or have an accident they come immediately'.

Harry said, 'Hold your horses, Lena. We're still capable of fending for ourselves; we're not geriatric yet'.

'You don't tell them that, you dozy bastard. Let them think I need round-the-clock care'. Lena read the letter again. 'Do you think they allow dogs? What about Yellow? We could never leave him; he's part of the family'.

Harry said when he was filling in the forms it asked about pets, and it didn't seem to be a problem. But they could confirm that when they went to visit.

Harry and Lena said in unison, 'Thank goodness we're getting out of this shithole!'

Yellow barked twice.

'Even the mutt agrees', Harry said with a laugh.

*

Nobby and Willie were into week six of their Nordic cruise, and it was spectacular; they were being treated like royalty. A steward arrived in the mornings with Earl grey tea on a silver tray. In the evenings, when they returned to their suite, their bed had been turned down and chocolates placed on their pillows.

Willie thought he'd died and gone to heaven. He was going to make the most of this trip and milk it dry.

Nobby's stress levels had gone down to normal level; what a good idea this cruise had been. They had already dined at the captain's table at least five times, and he noticed a few envious stares from fellow passengers.

Nobby was slightly bothered about the attention Captain Felix had been giving Willie (he was flirting with him), and it was obvious he batted for the other side.

Willie smiled as he was soaking up the sun on deck, having a quiet time away from Nobby. Nobby had dashed down to the medical bay to get some sea sickness pills. *Why would he book a cruise if he didn't have sea legs?* Willie was lucky he loved the swell and drop off the ship; it was soothing to him. With a bit of luck, Nobby might be incapacitated most of the trip.

That would give Willie the freedom to flirt openly with Captain Felix. They had seemed to hit it off right away, and they had a lot in common—similar age for one, and they loved to party and let their hair down.

Nobby unfortunately didn't have any hair to let down and was a party pooper to boot. Willie didn't think the captain had a partner, not according to the cabin crew; Willie had been picking their brains casually to get as much info as possible. *I suppose if you spend most of your life cruising up and down, always on duty, you'd have to have a very understanding partner, just like me,* Willie thought.

Nobby was looking green around the gills. He had no idea he would feel so sick, reacting so badly to the ebb and flow of the ship. He'd gratefully accepted the opportunity of an injection; the pills just weren't strong enough. But the unfortunate effects were to make you sleepy, so he'd had to go lie down for a few hours.

He was worried Willie would get up to mischief if he weren't around to keep an eye on him.

*

Gabby had sneaked around to Jeff's as soon as it became dusk. Jeff was a little surprised to see her.

Gabby asked if she could come in away from prying eyes.

Jeff ushered her in and asked if she wanted a drink.

Gabby felt she needed a bit of Dutch courage and asked for a large glass of wine.

Jeff smiled. 'To what do I own the pleasure?'

Gabby downed her glass in one gulp. 'I've come to put a proposition to you that would benefit us both'.

Jeff looked at the empty glass. 'Would you like a refill?'

Gabby shook her head. 'I need to be sober to tell you what I have in mind'.

And off she went on a tangent, telling Jeff all about the camper van, what a great place it was, blah, blah, blah. Then she stopped for breath.

Jeff said, 'Are you sure you wouldn't like another drink? You seem really uptight, which isn't like you'.

Gabby sighed and said, 'Yes, I'd love another wine', before she could tell him what was bothering her.

As soon as Jeff disappeared into the kitchen, she smiled. This was working out just as she had planned it.

Jeff returned carrying the whole bottle of wine, which was by now only half full. He plonked it on the table for her to help herself.

'So what's eating away at you?' he asked.

'It's a delicate situation. I'm being stalked by Juan—he's making too many inappropriate advances towards me. I've told him I'm not interested, but he doesn't seem to take it on board. That's why I need to go away with you, so he would think he's missed his chance and back off'.

Jeff stroked his little goatee. 'I see. So I'm being used as a scapegoat in a way. I can see if it would put Juan off the scent, because nobody wants damaged goods, so to speak'.

Jeff was turning things over in his mind. This could be an opportunity to test the waters, see if they were compatible sharing a bed, confined to a small space. It would test their mettle, but it was only for two nights. 'I'm up for it. When do we leave?'

*

Elvira was impressed with how her chicken casserole had turned out. she only had to see the look of delight on Dicky's face, whilst he was wolfing it down.

Dicky had asked Elvira to share lunch together and had opened a bottle of plonk.

Elvira was happy to spend time alone with Dicky. Juan had left earlier to attend to another job.

Dicky cleared his throat after he'd polished off his third helping. *Here goes,* he thought, now or never to put his long-term plan to Elvira, painting a rosy picture of how their lives could pan out quite differently, to being in a comfortable rut. How starting afresh somewhere new could be the excitement they both needed, and to leave any unpleasant memories far behind them.

Elvira nearly choked on her wine. She was shocked and pleased at the same time, and she didn't need to flirt or engage round two. She was lost for words. She'd never thought for one moment what Dicky was proposing could be happening to her. Elvira blushed, not usually like her to be coy.

'Dicky', she said,' I'm overwhelmed. It's like a dream-come-true. The only hesitation I have is love me, love my cats. I can't desert them—where I go, they go'.

Dicky smiled and said, 'Don't worry. I've already come up with a plan'. He then went off about their future, which included her pussies.

*

Jimmy was compiling all the information he had researched regarding counselling, AA meetings, even down to how to get rid of unwanted flab. Liposuction seemed to be a popular one, but it didn't curb people's appetites. Apparently, you put twice as much back on in a different place, not ideal. Laparoscopic gastric banding surgery, followed by abdominoplasty (tummy tuck) sounded a much better option. However, it was the most expensive. But in the long run, what he could save in grocery and booze bills he could afford to pay a regular sum every month on his visa.

Jimmy's only other task now was to grab the bull by the horns and approach Cassie with all this info— and what the alternative would be if she refused, him doing a walkabout. He had better hide the gin bottles and glassware from her before he commenced with what would be a life-changing experience for them.

Cassy had been nodding off outside in the sunshine, enjoying the heat penetrating her aching joints. It never entered her mind that if she lost weight, her joints wouldn't be under such stress. She was just rubbing Fiery Jack into her kneecaps when she espied Jimmy coming towards her. She quickly hid the tube down the side of the chair. She didn't want Jimmy putting two and two together.

Jimmy plonked himself down opposite Cassy, sighed, and said, 'We need to have a serious talk'.

Cassie gave Jimmy a hard stare. 'I hope you're not about to confess to a hidden affair or I won't be responsible for my reactions, but I know I'll make you suffer somehow'.

Jimmy shot back, 'No. It's far more serious than that, and I need you to keep your big mouth shut just for once and let me do all the talking. Your turn will come to say your bit soon enough'.

Cassy gasped. In all their married life, Jimmy had never spoken to her like that. She felt near to tears but would not give him the satisfaction of seeing her cry, a sign of weakness.

Jimmy placed all his paperwork on the table, told Cassie what it contained, stood up, and said, 'I shall be gone for a few hours to give you time to digest it all; you're bound to be in shock. I'm giving you space to think seriously about what the alternative would be to me leaving'.

Jimmy shot off down the decking before Cassie had time to draw breath.

*

Javier was taking his stage makeup off when there was a loud knock on his so-called dressing room door. *I hope it's not autograph seekers. I'm not in the mood; I'm feeling a little melancholy.*

Javier shouted, 'Come in!'

In came Margot, his agent, accompanied by a middle-aged gent in expensive Ralph Lauren chinos and polo shirt.

Margot smiled at Javier. 'This is Alan Spelling. He'd like to talk to you about a proposition'.

Javier got excited. He knew Alan by reputation as a successful director.

Javier held out his hand and shook it warmly. 'Hola, Mr Spelling. To what do I owe the pleasure?'

Alan's smile was genuine. He said, 'I'm impressed with your performance in *Priscilla, Queen of the Desert*, and I must congratulate you on your colourful, tasteful costumes, which Margot tells me you design yourself'.

Javier clapped his hands. 'I'm so glad someone appreciates my talents, Mr Spelling'.

'Call me Alan. I won't take up too much of your time. I know you are a busy man. I would like to offer you the leading role of Madam La Bain in my next play, *The French Follies*. The rehearsals take place in October, which gives you plenty of time to finish the pantomime'.

Javier gasped.

Alan continued. 'You would be expected to design your outfits again, and all costs will be covered. If you agree, we can discuss the financial details with you and

Margo over dinner tonight at the Admiral Hotel, shall we say 7pm prompt? I'm sure you'll be pleased with the offer we'll make. Until this evening then, Javier. Margo will escort me out'.

Javier's mouth dropped open as soon as they'd gone. At last, this was the opportunity he was destined for. He knew he was too talented to be doing pantomime to half-drunk tourists. He would be there tonight to accept whatever offer was on the table—anything was better than this existence.

*

Pedro was tucking into a full fry up, courtesy of Sammy, and he was feeling smug. He had Sammy under his spell again. She couldn't do enough for him. He'd made every effort to be nice to her, given her compliments of her cooking, even given her fifty euros to treat herself to a new hairdo.

He'd asked Sammy in a sad voice if she could possibly see her way to collecting all his belongings from the trailer park. He said Juan would help her. He was afraid to go himself to avoid unwanted nasty confrontations.

Pedro had asked Juan if he would box up his laptop and any porno lying around and make sure to seal it well. He didn't want Sammy seeing anything like that, or all his hard work would go down the drain. He'd spent all day yesterday filling in application forms, told a load of lies to impress them, so he stood a good chance of getting a position.

Pedro had suggested nicely that he and Sammy get established in their new working environment before they even consider marriage.

Sammy had agreed and said, 'It makes sense to be settled in before planning a wedding somewhere exotic'.

Good luck with that one, Pedro thought.

15

L**UCINDA WAS ADMIRING** her new red velvet drapes that Roberto had just hung in the bay window of their lounge, after lots of huffing and puffing and umpteen cups of coffee to keep him buzzing.

She loved living in the bungalow. The neighbours were nice—not like those interfering busybodies back at the trailer park. She'd spent a few lovely afternoons in their pristine little garden just soaking up the sun in her new sun lounger, complete with recliner.

Lucinda hadn't wasted any time at all with the decorating and refurbishment. Roberto and she had splashed out on a new dining table plus four chairs. It was sheer luxury to have the room in which to place one, no more TV dinners on their knees. She shuddered at the images of the tin hut they'd called home.

Roberto was splashing magenta satin paint on the kitchen walls. Thank goodness he'd managed to finish the living room to Lucinda's taste, which wasn't easy, seeing she changed her mind so often. He'd given Lucinda free choice everywhere, anything for a 'quiet' life. Although he had put his size tens down on having a mirrored ceiling in the bedroom, it would have resembled a brothel (not that he knew what a brothel looked like).

Roberto was so grateful to his mum for allowing them to live there, with so much space to fill, and Lucinda was doing a good job of filling it, maxing out his credit card. He wasn't getting any younger, and Lucinda had him working round the clock like a robot. He kept reminding her that Rome was not built in one day. He had a sneaking suspicion Lucinda had an ulterior motive for wanting everything done yesterday.

Lucinda shouted from the living room, 'I think our waterbed has arrived. A delivery van is backing up our drive. You'd better get out there fast. I don't want it damaged; it cost a lot of money'.

Roberto said to himself, 'Don't I know it. I'm the sucker that paid for it'.

Lucinda had nagged and nagged about buying it, saying it would improve not only their sleeping pattern but would be more romantic. Which in Roberto's eyes meant more interaction between the sheets, and maybe the ice maiden might melt at last, so a waterbed it was.

The bed had been erected, filled up to the correct limit, but it had to be left overnight to build up the right temperature before it could be comfortably used. Luckily, they had put their bed in the spare bedroom, which was bigger than the one they had in the tin hut.

Lucinda had gone to a lot of trouble to cook Roberto his favourite meal, steak a la chips, with a generous helping of pepper sauce. She thought Roberto had worked hard so deserved to be treated as a one off. Lucinda wasn't going to tell Roberto she was proud of him obtaining this bungalow and providing new fixtures and fittings exactly to her taste. She didn't want it sending out the wrong signals. Treat them mean and keep them keen was her motto.

Roberto tucked into his succulent steak, and gave an, 'Ooh, that's delicious, Lucinda. What are you trying to hide from me?' This had guilt written all over it, the last supper for a condemned man.

Lucinda smiled and said, 'Let's have a toast to our new home and life'.

They raised their glasses and said, 'Cheers'.

'Oh, before I forget', she said, 'Joyce and Jacques will be coming over for a meal on Friday. Would you be kind enough to pick up some caviar and champagne on your way home on Thursday?'

Roberto groaned and thought, *That's the hidden agenda and Lucinda's motto—keeping up appearances.*

*

Yellow was rushing round and round, barking at leaves blowing in the garden. He was so excited to have his own dirt to dig up, and he could bury his bones for a rainy day. He went bounding over to his owners for his tummy tickling.

Lena was enjoying her third G&T with her magazine gossip weekly open on her lap. She'd just read an article about Sundown Casino on the main strip in Altea, which had been raided by the local policia on Saturday last. Apparently, they had found a secret room in the basement, which was being used as a pole dancing brothel.

Lena had a vague recollection of Harry mentioning him and his mate, Stan the man, popping in on a regular occasion for a quick drink and a game of backgammon. *Is that too much of a coincidence?* she thought. Harry had a healthy appetite for sex, but she didn't. The thought of his hot, hairy, overweight torso on top of her repulsed her. She loved Harry but more in the way of brotherly love and companionship.

In a way, she should be relieved. If he was getting his oats elsewhere, he'd be less inclined to pester her.

'But wait a minute' she said. 'If they've closed it down, that's not looking good for me'.

Harry had shouted at Yellow to stop digging up so much dirt, or he'd have the stickler of a warden on his back. They were community gardens, after all.

Harry was content to be living in their one-bed condo on the ground floor, giving them access straight to the garden. What a pleasant contrast to the shitty trailer park. He and Lena didn't miss it or any of the other residents one little bit.

This was their perfect little haven, and the only fly in the ointment was the bad news Stan had conveyed to him on his mobile, about the shutting down of the casino. Shit, shit, what would they do now? he thought. Their regular Thursday night gamble and romp in the hay with Gina would be history.

Stan told Harry not to sweat, Gina had given him her private mobile number plus her address. Gina said she's going into business for herself, cutting out the middleman. She'd had a bellyful of pimps creaming off her hard-earned cash.

Harry said to Stan, 'But that's like prostitution, isn't it?'

'So what? It didn't bother you before'.

'Aye', said Harry. 'Let's hope her fees haven't gone up. I'll tell Lena we got fed up gambling and never winning, so we have decided to go to Luigi's cafe bar instead for a few jars and a friendly game of cards'.

'Will we still be going on Thursdays?'

Stan said, 'I'll have to get back to you on that'.

'OK, but remember, I can't do Wednesday, that's Lena's bingo night at the Palace Gardens. She won't give that up, and of course I have to accompany her, otherwise I dread to think what state she would get herself into, she needs me to get her home safely'.

'OK. Will be seeing you soon I hope'.

*

Jeff was exhausted in a good way. After two nights in the camper van with Gabby, he'd soon realised she was a vamp in the bedroom and a chef in the kitchen—what a combination. She was also good company, never a dull moment—they'd had lots of fun going out walking, eating al fresco, and collapsing into bed in the early hours of the morning. It didn't stop Jeff giving his all; he had lots of stamina. It was good to know he hadn't lost it. He was still a stud.

He was tucking into what would be their last lunch before heading back to their separate trailers. Jeff had decided life with Gabby would be good for him. He would suggest they go for a last stroll on the beach, call for a coffee somewhere, and then ask her if his plan of moving to Meadow Pastures would appeal to her. He felt confident her reply would be yes. Modesty had never been his strong point.

Gabby was having fun, grounding on the beach, laughing and chatting with Jeff. He was an easy person to be with; he oozed charm and charisma. Gabby wished they didn't have to go so soon, maybe they could stay a few more days. The camper was vacant until Friday. What did they have to go back for, living in their separate trailers sneaking around. The earth had moved for Gabby these past two nights. She wasn't ready to give that up just yet.

She'd ask Jeff what he thought of staying until Thursday. Gabby didn't want to visualise how going back to their separate lives would pan out.

She had to come up with a plan they could both commit to, something more permanent than an odd night or two. After all, the timing had to be right now for change.

Jeff returned with two lattes with iced donuts.

Gabby sputtered out, 'I don't want to go back to the trailer park yet. Can we stay a couple more nights, please? Money's no object. I've got my debit card with me, so we can eat out more, relax more'. *Not to mention more action in the bedroom*, she thought.

Jeff said, 'What a great idea. You sure it's OK with your sister?'

'Yes, perfect. Now what did you want to say?'

'I've been thinking about us maybe having a future together. We get on really well. I think we could have some fun in our old age. The only fly in the ointment is the trailers are too small for two people to occupy comfortably. Why don't we sell up and move to Meadow Pastures for over 60s? I think we fit the bill'.

Gabby shrieked, 'Oh, Jeff, that sounds wonderful! This is such a big step—what shall we do first?'

'We enjoy ourselves here, and in the meantime we'll contact the management to see if we can do a viewing before we return to our rabbit hutches. Selling our trailers will be our priority, after we put a deposit down on our new property'.

Gabby said, 'I'll take care of the deposit. After all, it's only money; you can't take it with you. There are no pockets in shrouds'.

Jeff smiled. *I've hit the jackpot with Gabby—a nymph with money—what more could a man want?*

*

Elvira and Dicky had now viewed plenty of converted barns in Altea Hills. They had narrowed it down to a two-bed upside-down humble homestead. The views were panoramic—mountains on one side and a long-distance sea view on the other. Totally private with one and a half acres of land, complete with olive and lemon trees, great for the felines too. The owner had accepted a lot lower offer because he was keen to sell. He was going through a tricky divorce, and the soon-to-be ex was milking him dry.

Dicky had been especially busy looking over the yearly turnover of the El Cid bar, situated on the prom overlooking the beach and sea. It had fifty covers, which would be ample. He didn't want anything too demanding. Doing simple tapas was ideal for the locals. He was going to keep Pueblo the chef to carry on with the food, everything else he and Elvira could manage. They would rent for a while with a view to purchase next year if the annual yield was adequate enough for him and Elvira to live comfortable on.

Elvira was on her way to meet up with Dicky at El Cid's to discuss their next move. Elvira had just finished her phone call to Timmy, the young lad who helped out at the pet shop, who was looking after her mini zoo until she returned. She had asked him not to tell Mr Moggie where she was or what she was planning, just in case things didn't go according to plan and she needed to keep earning.

Dicky and Elvira were exited at not only the prospect of a new home together but a business too.

Elvira had reservations about running a bar. She had no experience at all.

Dicky laughed and said to Elvira, 'You are a natural for any bar, just strut around looking sexy, we'll soon have the place rocking. Shall we take the plunge and sign up now?'

Two months later Elvira and Dicky were comfortably settled in their little love nest. She had been a little worried about relocating her pussies. But they had taken to their new environment like ducks to water. They loved the outdoor freedom, which they had never experienced before, sheer pussy heaven.

Dicky was pleased the bar was becoming popular with the locals all because they kept it Spanish cuisine, only tapas on the menu. Dicky was not going to make the same mistake most ex pats did, offering the usual crap of fish and chips and roast beef dinners. Why did holiday makers come to Spain to have Yorkshire pudding or Lancashire hot pot? Stay at home if you don't appreciate Spanish cooking. The bonus was Elvira waiting on customers dressed in her spray-on shorts and miniscule boob tube, which probably explained why most of the punters were male.

Cassie was eagerly awaiting an email reply from her sister, Sissy, who ran a small hotel in Barcelona. Her husband of twenty-five years had sadly passed away from a brain tumour three months ago. Jimmy and she had attended the funeral. They'd flown over for a long weekend because Sissy had needed her support. Sissy's son, Emanuel, 22, was a great help. He ran the business side and was a whiz with technology, knew all the best sites to advertise their hotel, so they were always booked well in advance.

Cassy had emailed Sissy last week, telling her all about Jimmy's unrealistic terms. She asked if she could come and stay for a while to give Jimmy a taste of his own medicine. See how he liked being left first. He'd soon be begging her to return.

The computer pinged. It was Sissy replying. Cassy felt a bit nervous, but she opened the email.

Sissy had gushed about how sorry she was and what a cad Jimmy was being. She told Cassy to pack her bags straightaway. She would have Emanuel pick her up at the airport and drop her off at her two-bed condo. Emanuel, she said, lived at the hotel to be on call if need be. Sissy said she could do with the company; she was lonely since Fernando had passed away.

Cassy wasted no time and got straight on to Ryanair's website and booked her one-way flight next morning at 11am. She paid for the ticket with Jimmy's credit card, which would make his eyes water, she thought. Next, she booked a taxi to get her to the airport, and she made sure she'd booked wheelchair assistance at the airport. No queuing for her, straight through to the bar for a few drinks to relax before the flight. She wasn't too keen on flying. The seats were never wide enough, she was always wedged in, and she couldn't move.

Luckily, Jimmy had texted her a couple of hours ago to say he was staying at the Duke of Wellington Pub overnight to give her more space to mull things over. All she needed to do now was sort out her packing and write a letter for Jimmy. She would have loved to see his face when he read it.

Cassy heaved her bulk out of the chair and headed inside. *I'll just make myself a G&T first to settle my nerves before heaving that suitcase down from the wardrobe.*

*

Jimmy looked round the small room he'd booked for the night. It would suffice if was clean and had an en-suite. The bar was just downstairs, with a small bistro, were he had booked a table for tonight for his evening meal. Yes, what more could a bloke want? No nagging wife—he was going to enjoy every minute of this.

He was tempted to stay for a week, but Cassy would be on the warpath for sure. He reluctantly agreed with himself to return home tomorrow afternoon and face her wrath.

Jimmy thoroughly enjoyed his calamari and potato bravas, washed down with a pint of local brew. He knew he'd have at least two more before staggering up to bed. Sleep came quicker if you were slightly tipsy.

*

Jimmy woke about 9.30am. The sun was streaming through the gaps in the blinds. He heaved himself out of bed and staggered into the bathroom for a cold shower to blow away the cobwebs and ease his thumping head.

After demolishing a hearty breakfast and feeling like a condemned man, he decided to go for a long walk on the beach, do some grounding, clear his head. Get ready for the sparring match he knew he was bound to face.

*

Arriving back at the trailer, he was a little surprised to find the door locked and no Cassy sat like a beetroot outside in her usual chair. He fished out his keys and entered the kitchen, which was none too tidy. Dirty dishes were piled in the sink, empty glasses on the coffee table.

The first thing Jimmy noticed was a brown envelope propped up against the kettle. He couldn't believe what he was reading, Cassy had been vitriolic with her words, but the gist of it was she was staying with Sissy for the near future. Sissy needed her help, and she would not return until he came to his senses and sent her an apology—in other words to crawl back on all fours.

Jimmy said to himself, 'I can't believe my luck'. Cassie had cut off her nose to spite her face. Hell would freeze over before he offered any apologies. He'd have the trailer all to himself. Firstly, he had to cancel his joint account, see how Cassy coped with that. Let her use her own money for booze or scrounge of Sissy. Either way he would be financially sound. Secondly, he would change the lock on the door, just in case.

I wonder what Kelly is doing tonight, he thought. *I think I'll give her a text see if she fancies meeting up for a drink and a bite to eat.* Life was looking a lot rosier now. Jimmy was humming as he reached for his phone.

*

Nobby was feeling quite ill. He didn't think it was sea sickness. He had pains in his chest and difficulty breathing. He reached out to shake Willie awake.

Willie groaned and opened one eye. 'What time is it? What did you wake me up for?'

Nobby wheezed. 'Go get help. I think I'm having a heart attack'.

Willie jumped out of bed and grabbed the phone. After a few beeps the steward answered.

Willie managed to garble into the phone about needing the ship's doctor right away, it was an emergency.

After the doctor examined Nobby, he took Willie over to one side and said, 'We have to get Nobby down to sick bay, he needs an oxygen mask to help with his breathing, I think he's suffered a stroke'.

Once Nobby had been settled as comfortably as possible with an oxygen mask on, he drifted into a deep sleep.

The doctor said, 'We need to keep him under observation, Nurse Mary will be here with him, There's nothing more you can do Willie, he's in good hands'.

Willie couldn't wait to get upstairs on deck. He needed fresh air to get rid of the smell of the sick bay.

Whatever would they do now? There were still four days left of the cruise, and it was very unlikely Nobby would be in any state to enjoy them.

Willie felt sorry for him, but it was mixed with a sense of relief that he didn't have to give him round-the-clock care; he was in the best place for him.

Nobby was conscious but in a lot of pain, therefore Captain Felix had organised to put into the nearest port, Barcelona, so Nobby could disembark and be taken to the De La Santa Cruz hospital.

Captain Felix escorted Willie off the ship and shook his hand, 'I hope Nobby will be ok Willie' he said. The paramedics had already placed Nobby inside the Ambulance.

Willie was talking hesitantly to Nobby whilst they were travelling, saying how grateful he was about the cruise, and how he was looking forward to organising another one, as soon as Nobby recovered. Nobby drifted in and out of consciousness, unable to speak coherently, just to give a weak smile to Willie.

Nobby after several hours became fully awake, Willie informed Nobby he would be staying overnight in a small room just down the corridor from him.

Willie was awoken just after 7.00 am by a nurse knocking on his door. Willie quickly opened the door, the nurse told him to follow her, telling him the doctor needed to see him urgently.

The doctor ushered Willie into Nobby's room, Nobby was hooked up to a heart monitor which was beeping spasmodically. Willie gasped 'what's happened doctor' he said.

The doctor sighed and replied 'I'm so sorry Willie, but I'm afraid Nobby has suffered a heart attack, the nurse said he had struggled with her to get out of bed in confusion of where he was. The nurse tried to restrain him, but he fell out of bed, and I think the shock was too much for Nobby's weak heart to cope with'.

'Is Nobby still alive, will he recover' asked Willie.

I think the best thing for Nobby now, is for you to stay with him and if you are a religious man, pray for him. Meanwhile the nurse will be keeping a close watch on Nobby's monitor' said the doctor.

Nobby took his last breath a couple of hours after Willie had been holding his hand. Nobby was in shock, he knew the tears would come later, when reality hit home.

The journey home from the hospital gave him time to digest everything properly. They would have to perform an autopsy on Nobby before any death certificate could be issued. Willie knew everything would be covered by the insurance policy Nobby had taken out. It was as if he'd had a premonition about his fate before they even set sail.

*

A month after Nobby' funeral, which was sparse because he didn't have any living family, and friends were few and far between.

Willie received a letter from Captain Felix sending his condolences, and he had enclosed a brochure of a cruise around the Mediterranean. Captain Felix would be sailing in three weeks, and he'd invited Willie to take advantage of joining him and a few friends, gratis. *It might help you with your grieving process. You'd have your own quarters, no sharing involved. It would be my pleasure if you could join us.*

Willie was stunned. He'd done the crying and feeling sorry for himself bit. The time was right to get on with his life. Nobby would want that. Nobby, bless him, had left Willie quite comfortably off. What an opportunity; he couldn't believe his luck.

Willie said out loud, 'Holla Marinero, (hello Sailor) here I come'.

*

Javier had been given a grand tour round Benidorm Palace, where he would be performing five nights a week for the next six months. He was impressed with the sheer glamour and glitz of the place. It suited his personality to perfection.

Javier had been booked into the new Flash Hotel, and he had a suite to himself with a lounge, master bedroom plus en-suite, and a balcony with jacuzzi. He had been assigned a nice young man, Nick, to be his righthand man. Nick had an adjoining room to Javier's. He would take care of his laundry and help out with Javier's costumes. Nick apparently was a whiz with a needle.

Nick had introduced Javier to the rest of the cast, who were very professional. They welcomed Javier with genuine warmth, no jealousies or hostility at all.

Javier was basking in the attention he was getting when Nick dragged him away to be introduced to the backstage crew, who were just as important as the actors; without them, there would be no show.

Nick said to everyone in the room, 'We have all been invited to a private party down in the function room tonight at 7pm, as an ice-breaking get-together'.

Opening night came around far too quickly for Javier, who was nervous. He knew his costumes were magnificent, and he could recite his lines backwards, but he still got first-night butterflies in his tummy.

After curtain call, Javier and the cast received a standing ovation. The local rag the next day had stated what a great show, with amazing performers, very professional. But the star of the show was the newcomer Javier, a showstopper. When he sang, you could hear a pin drop. He was bound to go far, and this was just the start of his career. The world was his oyster.

Javier had tears in his eyes when he read the review. He said, 'Trailer trash, watch this space and eat your hearts out'.

*

Pedro and Sammy had successfully relocated their sparse belongings to their new log cabin, situated in one of Estepona's trailer parks. Their duties at the site office would not commence until next Monday, which gave them plenty of time to get organised. Luckily, the cabin came fully furnished. Pedro was impressed, he hadn't expected such decent living quarters, with really good quality fittings. He was used to second-hand, rundown castoffs at the other trailer park.

Sammy had been over the moon and couldn't thank Pedro enough for this opportunity given to them for a new life.

Pedro and Sammy were sightseeing to explore the lovely resort they would now call home. It was picture perfect, clean and full of life. Pedro couldn't wait to frequent all the bars and cafes dotted all over the place. There was even a casino open twenty-four hours, which he'd be frequenting given half a chance.

He knew he had to play it carefully to begin with, be attentive, work hard. The day would eventually come when he could slip into his old ways and habits, without Sammy knowing. Lull her into a false sense of security, get her fully trapped by the new him, and then bingo, time to experience Estepona's babes.

Sammy was wondering when the timing would be right to break it gently to Pedro. He was about to become a father, not once but twice (a scan had confirmed it was twins).

They would be able to manage just fine, she thought. After all, she was only taking care of the admin side of the trailer park. Pedro was doing all the rest—repairs and keeping the place spic and span.

Between work and fatherly duties, Pedro would be too knackered to return to his old ways of boozing and womanising.

Sammy chuckled and said, 'I can't wait to see his face when I tell him. He'll be so excited and proud'.

16

TWENTY TRAILERS USED to occupy the Trailer Trash Havana Park. Not anymore. The owner, Mr Maitland, had repurchased all twenty units and paid the residents the going rate at the time.

He then sold out for a healthy price to Happy Gardens Holiday Camp.

Within no time, ten log cabins complete with their own Jacuzzis had been erected. It was now a small, fun park catering to families with young children, even had a creche. Non-residential holiday lets only.

Dicky's old bistro and Gustave's bar was now just one big jungle themed cafe/bar, attracting families with rug rats, a bit like Disney Land.

There was also a water park complete with a lake and pedal boats.

All in all, a really tasteful and good value for your money, an all-inclusive holiday destination. It was popular with the Brits and Dutch.

Do you think any of the residents who used to reside here were ever tempted to spend a holiday there, just for the sheer nostalgia?

I wonder.

CPSIA information can be obtained
at www.ICGtesting.com
Printed in the USA
LVHW111953130921
697726LV00006B/1050

9 781728 379258